CUMBRIA LIBRARIES

KT-178-122

3 8003 05164 8772

HAMISH
AND THE
NEVERPEOPLE

For Alfie, Joshua and George
The Carruthers Rotters
Danny Wallace

For my brother Paul, the one-man band.
Jamie Littler

First published in Great Britain
in 2016 by Simon & Schuster UK Ltd
A CBS COMPANY
Text copyright © 2016 Danny Wallace
Illustrations copyright © 2016 Jamie Littler
Design by Paul Coomey

This book is copyright under the Berne Convention.
No reproduction without permission.
All rights reserved.
The right of Danny Wallace and Jamie Littler to be identified as the author and
illustrator of this work respectively has been asserted by them in accordance
with sections 77 and 78 of the Copyright, Design and Patents Act, 1988.

7 9 10 8
Simon & Schuster UK Ltd
1st Floor, 222 Gray's Inn Road
London
WC1X 8HB

www.simonandschuster.co.uk
Simon & Schuster Australia, Sydney
Simon & Schuster India, New Delhi
A CIP catalogue record for this book is available from the British Library.
PB ISBN 978-1-4711-2391-7
eBook ISBN 978-1-4711-2392-4

This book is a work of fiction. Names, characters, places and incidents are
either the product of the author's imagination or are used fictitiously.
Any resemblance to actual people living or dead, events or locales
is entirely coincidental.

Printed and bound by CPI Group (UK) Ltd, Croydon, CR0 4YY
Simon & Schuster UK Ltd are committed to sourcing paper that is made from wood
grown in sustainable forests and supports the Forest Stewardship Council, the
leading international forest certification organisation. Our books displaying
the FSC logo are printed on FSC certified paper.

HAMISH
AND THE NEVERPEOPLE

BY DANNY WALLACE
ILLUSTRATED BY JAMIE LITTLER

SIMON & SCHUSTER

LONDON NEW YORK SYDNEY TORONTO NEW DELHI STARKLEY

Starkley

17nd Thursday 2016 issue XXX vol 8

WORLDSTOPPERS VANQUISHED IN STARKLEY

Hamish hailed a hero!

The WorldStoppers are officially gone, according to local policeman Saxon Wix, who's had a really good look around.

'It's all thanks to Hamish Ellerby and the PDF,' added PC Wix.

The WorldStoppers – the evil monsters who could control time and 'freeze' everyone in Starkley so they could carry out their evil business – represented the biggest threat to humanity since reality television.

For his efforts, Hamish received a £10 book token and a forty second free sweet dash courtesy of Madame Cous Cous's International World of Treats (gobstoppers not included).

'At last we relax!' said PC W looking visibly re lieved and putting a Panda onesie.

FULL ST RY INSID

inside. p11

ost

PRICE £90p

news&cookers

R. DIDDUMS
For the fashion-conscious baby

"We specialise in baby berets!"

GBC

Life's a Dream with
Vapidia Sheen
On tonight's episode:
Vapidia avoids a
puddle
7.30pm - only on GBC

Pre

MA

dis

P

Sl

AS ANYBODY EEN MY OTTOM?

Local shoe magnate appy Tick has bought me new jeans – but esn't know what his bottom looks like in them.

'Every time I look myself in the mirror, I n only see what I look ke from the front. I think must be broken. It just on't show me my bottom!'

Mr Tick is appealing or members of the public shout out when they can e his bottom, 'so that can turn around really uickly and see it for myelf. I simply must see my ottom!'

Thursday 2015 vol 8 issue XXX

Starkley Post

BELASKO

Making matches, tiles, bricks, medicine, footballs and whatnot since The Before.

PRIME MINISTER HEADED TO TOWN

Prime Minister Ernst Ding-Batt, the tallest prime minister in fifty years, has announced his plans to visit Starkley.

'I am the tallest prime minister in fifty years!' he said in a statement. 'And I am the only one to have owned a poodle!'

The last celebrity to visit Starkley was Jonny Bingo, owner of Britain's smallest tractor, who arrived in 2004 after taking a wrong turn at Frinkley.

ANOTHER POTATO

MYSTERIOUS WOMAN SPOTTED

A mysterious woman was spotted in town recently.

'She was dressed all in white,' said Gum Spittle, 85. 'But she didn't look like a dentist. I suppose that's why she looked so mysterious.'

The news comes just six months after a strange ship marked HMS CARRAS was seen down by the cliffs.

'Maybe she was a sailor who got lost,' suggested Ms Spittle, who then tripped and fell over an onion.

You Nitwit!

Oh, dear.

What HAVE you done?

You picked up this book and started reading, didn't you?

You've read three sentences already.

And now you've read four!

Oh, that is unfortunate.

You should stop right now because you need to be made of tough stuff to handle what's coming.

I'm serious. Just stop right now.

Because are you ready to learn about something that will change your life forever?

Are you ready to find out one of the biggest secrets in the world?

Something so big and so secret that this is literally the only book on the planet that knows about it?

Even if it means putting yourself . . . in danger?

Because out there, somewhere in the world, plans are being made.

Huge plans, so evil and so dastardly that you'd be better off putting this book down immediately and doing whatever it is you normally do with your time. Licking kittens. Putting socks on your ears. Stinking up the place.

Oh, it doesn't matter who you are or what your name is. It doesn't matter how tough you think you are. You need to be prepared!

Once, a tough kid with the tough name of Belch Sting read this book. Do you know what happened to Belch Sting straight after? His feet fell off. They had to use the wheels from an old office chair to replace his feet, and now he just trundles around, looking sad. You should have seen him trying to walk upstairs at night. His parents had to install a ski lift.

After him, a girl called Runt Sneer had a go. It might even have been this very copy of the book. Well, it blew her mind. I mean literally. A small wisp of smoke puffed from both ears and now all she can talk about is shoelaces.

Is that really what you want to happen to you?

I didn't think so. I'll give you one last chance.

You should stop reading RIGHT NOW if you don't want to know that the people of Earth are in big, big trouble.

Like – huge trouble.

Oh, come on – where's your imagination? *Double* what you're thinking.

Because the person making those evil and dastardly plans I was talking about? The one who is stalking around, coming up with dreadful ideas? The one who might well be outside your house right this very second? Well, that person has plans for an apocalypse so big you might as well call it a MEGAPOCALYPSE.

And if you keep reading . . . well, that person will know that you are just like Hamish Ellerby, of 13 Lovelock Close, Starkley.

That person will know that, like Hamish, you are brave enough to keep going even when the threats pile up.

That makes you dangerous.

So now you have a decision to make.

Turn the page, and start to discover the secrets, even if that means your feet might fall off.

Or close this book and run away screaming while you can.

Buzzing!

The small town of Starkley was buzzing.

The TV vans were arriving. They had huge satellite dishes on top, and people with clipboards inside. They snaked into town, past the big, boring, beige Starkley sign, and parked up outside Winterbourne School.

The town had been on TV once or twice before, of course.

It had been on *Britain's Most Boring Towns*.

It had been on *100 Places You'll Probably Never Go*.

And, thanks to the efforts of Hamish Ellerby and his friends just a couple of weeks earlier, it had even been on *Whoa! This Random Little Place Actually Saved the World!*

But today was different. Now Starkley was being invaded by television cameras because the Prime Minister was coming.

When he'd announced it, the Prime Minister hadn't even really seemed sure where Starkley was.

'We shall be filming an episode of *Question Me Silly* in . . .

er . . . Starkley,' he'd said on TV one night. 'Which is . . . a place. With people who live in that place. And all manner of other things, I imagine, such as a local shop, most probably, and a bench of some sort.'

No one had been surprised that the Prime Minister knew so little about Starkley. Until it had hit the headlines recently, even people who lived there sometimes weren't exactly sure where Starkley was. They just knew it was where they kept all their stuff. Nowadays, though, they were actually rather proud of it.

You see, just a few months ago, Starkley had been at the centre of a potential worldwide disaster! Evil beasts called the WorldStoppers had invaded the town along with their awful friends the Terribles. They'd found a way of making the whole world 'Pause' and had stolen grown-ups, made people grumpy and generally tried to cause as much havoc as possible in the hope of taking over the world. But, luckily for the world, Hamish and his friends had been immune to the Pause and created an uprising to stop the monsters from taking over. So, little old boring Starkley that no one had ever really noticed before suddenly became a lot more interesting. And Hamish and the Pause Defence Force (the **PDF**) had

become local celebrities.

Now, as Hamish walked through the town square filled with sunflowers, he could see that everybody was just hanging around, hoping to be filmed.

Mr Slackjaw had polished all the beautiful mopeds lined up in a row outside Slackjaw's Motors.

Hamish's friend Robin had spent the morning making sure his football was fully inflated because he'd hate to be immortalised on television holding an under-inflated ball.

Astrid Carruthers had blow-dried her dog, so that it now looked three times its original size.

'Afternoon, Hamish!' said Mr Longblather, his teacher, smiling a broad smile, just in case a camera might be there to catch it. He'd waxed his moustache and ironed his tie.

'Oh! Hello, Hamish!' said Grenville Bile, who for the first time this year had combed his hair and was doing his best to sound super polite, even though he still had one finger jammed up a nostril as usual. 'I do hope you are enjoying this weather what we're having!'

Everyone was very keen for Starkley to make a good impression. Someone had even Blu-tacked a new sign to the town clock that read:

7

STARKLEY TOWN COUNCIL

To activate the speaking clock, simply stand here and say what the time is out loud.

Madame Cous Cous had spent the whole morning polishing the outside of Madame Cous Cous's International World of Treats. She'd arranged a whole new window display: Sweets of the Ocean. But all she'd really done was spread fish paste over some gobstoppers, which everyone agreed was actually pretty disgusting.

'It's supposed to look like frogspawn!' she yelled at everyone who passed, waving her stick around wildly. 'It's supposed to look **glamorous!**'

'Hamish!' said Dr Fussbundler, the dentist, walking out of the shop with his daily armful of Dundee Drizzle Balls. 'You must be excited! All this fuss – and all because of you!'

It was true. The Prime Minister had thought it would be a good idea to meet Hamish Ellerby – the otherwise unremarkable ten-year-old boy who'd managed to save the world.

The letter had been very posh...

Dear Hamish Ellerby,

It is I, the Prime Minister.

You can tell from my fancy handwriting that I'm very important. I would like to thank you and your friends on behalf of the whole country for saving us from the WorldStoppers and so on, etc., etc.

I intend to come to Starkley to film an episode of Question Me Silly and I would like to get you on the programme!

Hamish's older brother Jimmy said he knew exactly why the Prime Minister wanted Hamish on the show. He said it was because Hamish would make the Prime Minister look good. Otherwise, why had he never bothered to come to Starkley before? Jimmy was fifteen and said he knew 'everything about politics and that actually'.

As Hamish walked on, he saw his friend Buster up ahead, serving ice creams from his ice-cream van with his mum. But, before he could get there, a pair of cherry-red army boots suddenly dangled into view from a tree in front of him, and a girl dropped from the branches.

'ALWAYS BE PREPARED!' shouted Alice, leaping into a karate pose.

Alice Shepherd was Hamish's best friend. She'd had a blue streak in her hair when they'd first met and she'd enlisted him to join the **PDF**. Now she'd changed it to a sort of bright turquose.

Turkwoyse.

Torkoyz.

A sort of aquamarine colour.

Alice was always telling Hamish he had to be prepared these days. She said she always was.

'Prepared for what?' Hamish would ask.

'Prepared for *anything*!' she'd reply, her eyes darting nervously around.

Alice said she felt on edge. Like she knew adventure was just around the corner. She didn't understand how Hamish had just sort of got on with life when the last adventure had ended.

Alice got a nut and pickle baguette out of her bag and took a bite.

'So have you thought any more about my idea?' she said, poking him in the arm as they walked.

'What idea?' said Hamish, innocently, though he knew exactly what she meant.

'The **LONDON** idea!' said Alice. 'Come on, Hamish, you know you want to. We speak to a strange woman who mentions your missing dad, then a mysterious bird appears with a note in its beak, and on that note is an address . . . Surely you want to go there and find out what's going on?'

Truth was, Hamish did. I mean, think about it. One minute he'd been standing there, in Starkley town centre, just the other day, and the next he'd been approached by the strange woman. And, as if that wasn't weird enough, moments later a small blackbird landed, holding a folded piece of card on which was written . . .

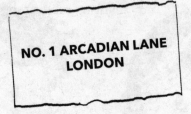

**NO. 1 ARCADIAN LANE
LONDON**

I mean – who wouldn't want to go there and find out more? But Hamish had responsibilities.

'Problem is, Alice, I've got my Saturday job at Slackjaw's Motors now,' he said. He liked working there. Mr Slackjaw was always telling him interesting facts. Did you know that when Henry Ford sold his very first Ford car, he told people,

'You can have *any* colour you like, so long as it's black!'? Hamish liked that. Although, since he'd told his mum, she'd started using the same trick.

'You can have anything you like for dinner,' she'd say, 'so long as it's sausage and mash!'

'Plus,' continued Hamish, 'Grenville is teaching me to wrestle on Tuesdays. And there's always so much to do at home. And then there's school, and—'

Alice bopped him on the head with her baguette.

'ALWAYS BE PREPARED!' she yelled. 'And you're running out of excuses, Hamish Ellerby. Personally, I think it's because you're scared.'

'I'm not scared!' said Hamish, rubbing his head, and finding a pickle there.

'You are,' said Alice. 'You're scared of what you might find out. You're scared of going to London because of what you might find out about your dad.'

And do you know what?

As she walked away, Hamish knew Alice was absolutely right.

Hamish hadn't seen his dad in six months now. Not since Boxing Day, when he'd popped out to buy ice cream and crisps in his sleek black Vauxhall Vectra and never returned.

Hamish had always thought a Vauxhall Vectra was quite a boring sort of car. The type that just blended in. These days, it was the only car he ever really looked out for.

This was the one great sadness in Hamish's life. His dad was brilliant. He was really tall and amazing at Boggle. When he'd disappeared, everyone had said how unlike him it was. Hamish had been worried his dad had just got bored of family life and left. But the mysterious woman who'd turned up in Starkley after the battle with the Terribles had told Hamish a few things about his dad.

That he was a hero.

That he was battling evil.

That he had knowledge others were after. That they were scared of him because he was the only one who could stop them.

And that he was helping 'the Neverpeople'.

Hamish didn't know who they were. What a strange name 'Neverpeople' was. And why was it up to his dad to help them? Hamish had always thought he was a salesman, not a top-secret spy or something . . . But the woman didn't tell Hamish what he really wanted to know: when – or if – his dad was coming back.

And then the blackbird had arrived, holding the address.

Somewhere deep inside, Hamish suspected his only chance of seeing his dad again was to follow that clue and go to No. 1 Arcadian Lane.

But, with life only just back to normal, did he really want to risk it all again? And was he brave enough? Did he really want to find out the truth? Because Hamish knew that sometimes the truth is scary.

In any case, there wasn't time to think about this now.

Everyone said, **'Ooh!'** as a fleet of six long black cars drove into Starkley.

The Prime Minister was here.

Going Live

Question Me Silly was one of those TV shows where they'd fill a school hall with angry-looking grown-ups sitting on small plastic chairs and say: 'We're about to turn the cameras on, so make sure you use loads of long words and pretend you're really furious about something or other, because all your friends and family will be watching and they'll think you're being important and clever!'

It was forty-five minutes long, but everyone agreed that it must be great value for money because it felt twice as long to watch.

At 6.55 p.m., Hamish queued with his mum, Jimmy and his friends to get into the hall. According to a poster on the wall, there were three important topics they'd be talking about on the show tonight.

Tonight's Three Important Topics (pay attention):

*The new potato-recycling scheme in Frinkley.
Should knitwear be banned
as a Christmas present?
Norway – where is it and what does it want?*

The show was hosted by Elydia Exma, a very snooty woman who was basically just a couple of nostrils on legs.

Elydia pretty much thought she was the cleverest and most brilliant person on the planet, which is why she always seemed to be looking over your head, as if her words deserved to be sent up into the heavens where they could be chiselled on to rocks and worshipped for all time, rather than wasted on your grubby little wax-filled ears.

She never looked people in the eye either. It was like she thought other people might wear some of her precious vision out. And what if someone better than the person she was talking to walked into the room?

Everyone had filed into the hall and taken their chairs.

Madame Cous Cous sat right at the front and handed out Cantonese Caramel Carbuncles.

People moved TV cameras about and got everything set up.

They said things like 'going live in two minutes' and 'can we check the satellite dish, please?'

Hamish sat right at the front too, between his mum and Jimmy. His friends Elliot and Clover, who'd helped him save the world from the WorldStoppers, took their seats behind him.

'Good luck, Hamish!' said Buster, patting him on the shoulder.

Hamish had been told that right at the end of the programme the Prime Minister would say a few words and make a fuss of him. Hamish's tummy flipped a little when he thought about it. His whole school would be watching.

And now here he was!

The Prime Minister himself strode in, hands clasped together over his head like a champion boxer, ready to take his seat.

Hamish studied him. Big, bushy, billowy, bristly beard like a Santa who'd just woken up. Little round glasses which made his eyes look even smaller than they were. The top of his head as round and pointy and bald as a pigeon's egg.

'He's so handsome!' cooed Madame Cous Cous.

The Prime Minister sat down. He was wearing a blue pinstriped suit and a bright green badge that read **PM OK!** (Everyone called him 'PM', which he thought was short for Prime Minister. In fact, they called him 'PM' because he never got up before noon.)

Hamish knew that Ernst Ding-Batt was a Prime Minister who was very keen for everybody to know just how brilliant his achievements were.

'I am the tallest Prime Minister in fifty years!' he'd tell anyone who'd listen, sometimes while banging his fist on a table. 'I am the only Prime Minister in the history of this country to own a poodle!'

'That's very impressive,' the people he kept around him would say, nodding to each other. 'We've definitely got the right chap here.'

'I can lift sixteen cans of Fanta at once!' he'd continue, pointing importantly in the air. 'I can say "excuse me, whose uncle is this?" in six different accents! I once fixed a broken pen using just my mind!'

That last one was his absolute favourite. It had been used a lot on posters when he was running for election.

We need a country in which pens can sometimes be mended just by thinking about how it would be better if they were mended

Anyway, it turned out that he didn't actually fix that pen – someone had just replaced it with one that worked and forgot to tell him. But no one minded much because he was still pretty tall and could lift all that Fanta.

But the PM didn't think any of this was odd at all. He treated his accomplishments as deadly serious. He was not one to laugh and joke around. What's more, he'd never travel anywhere without Mysterio, his personal life coach and executive assistant.

The most mysterious thing about Mysterio was how he got that job.

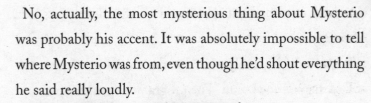

No, actually, the most mysterious thing about Mysterio was probably his accent. It was absolutely impossible to tell where Mysterio was from, even though he'd shout everything he said really loudly.

'AY-A AHM . . . MYSTERIO!' he'd yell, and people would think . . . *Italy maybe?*

'EET EEZ A NICE DAY!' he'd continue, and people would think . . . *France? Belgium?*

'UND NOW VEE MUST GO!' he'd finish, and people would think . . . *Germany? Sweden? Pluto?*

Mysterio's job was to walk around in a purple suit with

little silver stars on it, looking wise and mysterious, and then whispering in Mr Ding-Batt's ear. The only time he wasn't shouting was when he was whispering. It was like his volume control only had two settings: **CHURCH BELL LOUD** and *little old lady quiet*. Everyone assumed that when he whispered he was giving the Prime Minister excellent political advice. In reality, he was just whispering things he'd read off a motivational calendar he'd bought from a garage. *'Zee future eez now!'* he'd say, which is weird, isn't it? Because most people agree that the future's actually in a bit. *'Ownly by looging inzide yowself can you trulee zee inzide yowself!'* he'd whisper, and the Prime Minister would close his eyes and breathe deeply and nod slowly.

'Right!' said Elydia Exma. 'Cue the music!'

The theme tune began. The programme was starting!

But no one could have guessed that this would be the exact moment that something far more sinister started too.

3

Wait, What Just Happened?!

'Good evening and welcome to the programme, which this week comes from the hall of Winterbourne School in the small town of Starkley,' said Elydia Exma, her nose high in the air, but her beady little eyes fixed on the camera.

'Yes – *Starkley*,' continued Elydia, who managed to make everything she said sound like she was disgusted by it. It was as if she'd just found a sweaty sock in her minestrone soup, when she'd specifically asked for soup *without* one. 'Now Starkley is, of course, already a famous town . . .'

Proudly, Mr Longblather nudged PE teacher Tyrus Quinn in his enormous belly, which made Tyrus Quinn rumble and burp.

'It was the scene of a great triumph against some particularly evil monsters very recently,' said Elydia. 'But tonight we'll be talking about a new potato-recycling scheme instead.'

'Boo!' shouted a person in the audience. 'Down with potatoes!'

'With me on the panel,' continued Elydia, 'is local MP Shepton Mallet . . .'

'Hello!' grinned Shepton Mallet, looking into the wrong camera.

'We also have the Prime Minister, Ernst Ding-Batt . . .'

'Aloha!' said the Prime Minister very seriously. 'That's Hawaiian for hello.'

' . . . and the Prime Minister's special adviser, er . . . Mr Mysterio.'

'GREETINKS!' said Mysterio, and everyone in the audience thought, *Russia?*

Hamish felt another little quiver of excitement in his tummy. This was pretty cool.

'Prime Minister,' said Elydia, 'if I could start with you . . .'

'Well, first of all let me first say that I own a poodle,' said the Prime Minister. 'And I am in fact the only Prime Minister in the history of this country to actually own a poodle. And I think that's something I should just say from the very beginning.'

Someone started to applaud this, but then stopped quite quickly.

'Yes,' said Elydia, 'But about this potato-recycling scheme—'

'And what's more!' said the Prime Minister, standing up and making eye contact with the viewers at home. 'I once fixed a broken pen with the power of thought alone!'

'It was a different pen!' shouted someone in the audience.

'And, on the matter of this potato-recycling scheme, let me be *absolutely clear*,' continued Mr Ding-Batt. '*I am more than six feet tall in height!*'

He paused, dramatically, then sat back down again. Lots of people applauded and said, 'That's true, yes, he is.'

Elydia tapped her chin. She wasn't quite sure that he'd answered the question.

'Yes, but what do you think about the potato-recycling scheme?' she said.

The Prime Minister looked annoyed. Wasn't it enough that he was more than six feet tall in height?

Mysterio slid the Prime Minister a piece of paper, on which was written '*HERE EEZ WHAT TO SAY ABOOT THE POTATO-RECYCLING SCHEME*'. The Prime Minister stood up again and put on his most serious face.

'My thoughts on the potato-recycling scheme are as follows ...'

Hamish had been listening quite intently up until that point. It was pretty cool seeing the Prime Minister up close.

Normally, you only saw him on the news, standing in front of Big Ben, using words like 'economy', 'framework' and, of course, 'poodle'. But Hamish had been slightly distracted by something.

Because what *was* that he'd just felt? A slight judder? A slight creak in the room? He looked around to see if anyone else had noticed, but they were all just listening to the Prime Minister.

'Now look – potatoes are very important,' he was saying, very sincerely, but Hamish was distracted again. The spotlights had dimmed just a little. An electrician standing by a satellite dish looked up and scratched his head.

'. . . I myself enjoy potatoes,' said the PM.

'He's just like us!' whispered an old man to his wife.

'. . . whether mashed, roasted, in chip form or even just eating one raw, like one would an onion.'

Wait – was that another judder? Hamish could swear he felt the room rumble under his feet. He glanced at his friends, but they just stared straight ahead, listening to the Prime Minister's important words.

'I remember, as a child, I ate a potato,' said the PM, getting misty-eyed. 'These days I can eat up to eleven potatoes in one sitting.'

One thing was for certain: the Prime Minister was on fire! He had the audience in the palm of his hand. You could tell he was building up to something big.

'Which means that, on the matter of potato-recycling schemes, let me be *absolutely clear* . . .'

Everyone, including Elydia Exma, leaned forward to hear what the Prime Minister was about to say.

Everyone except Hamish, that is, because something just wasn't right with those lights. They weren't dimming any more . . . it was like they were slowly pulsating . . . getting brighter . . .

And *brighter* . . .

'And, just to be clear,' said the Prime Minister, enjoying the limelight, 'when I say I want to be absolutely clear, I clearly mean that I want to be *absolutely* clear when I say . . .'

PFZZZZZZ-POP

A spotlight popped.

Then another one! Tiny pieces of glass rained down on to the stage and tinkled about on the floor. But no one paid any attention. The room was silent. Hamish seemed to be the only person in Starkley not entranced by the Prime Minister's potato-based words. Everyone else was on the edge of their seats.

But Ernst Ding-Batt just stood there, suddenly seeming a little confused.

Had he forgotten his lines?

Mysterio pushed his little piece of paper forward with one finger again and coughed.

'Yes, Prime Minister?' said Elydia. 'What do you want to be absolutely clear about?'

The Prime Minister blinked, once.

What great words of wisdom was he about to impart?

And finally he said . . .

'I really like my little blue pants.'

No one said anything for a bit.

'I said **I REALLY LIKE MY LITTLE BLUE PANTS!**' yelled the PM. *'They're new!'*

That was a bit of an odd thing to say. Especially on live TV when you're supposed to be a serious Prime Minister.

'You . . . you really like your new pants?' said Elydia, struggling to believe her ears.

'Yes,' said the Prime Minister. 'I really like my new pants. They're proper comfy-womfy.'

Someone in the audience applauded this, confused.

'But . . . but I was asking you about potato recycling . . .' said Elydia, checking her notes. There were definitely no questions on there about the Prime Minister's pants.

'What do you mean potato?' asked the Prime Minister, scratching his beard. 'What's a potato?'

'What's a *potato*?' said Elydia, and then for no apparent reason the Prime Minister broke into a little dance.

'Here!' he shouted. 'Film this! Film me doing my New Pants Dance!'

Outside, ten minutes later, Hamish watched in quiet confusion as the Prime Minister was rushed into a big black Range Rover with tinted windows.

'EE'S A NOT FEELING LIKE A CHIT-CHATTYING!' yelled Mysterio, slamming the door of the car, and at least four people in the crowd thought, *Maybe he's Mexican?*

They'd stopped *Question Me Silly* early, saying the Prime Minister had been suddenly taken unwell, and put on an episode of *Life's a Dream with Vapidia Sheen* instead. They'd done it just in time. The Prime Minister had already done his New Pants Dance, then tried to eat a raw potato and finally dropped his trousers so he could show everyone just how proud he was of his brand-new undies. A tall man in a soldier's uniform and shiny black boots had immediately rushed him out of the school.

Mysterio had spotted Hamish looking up at him.

'Oh, yerz . . . Hamish,' he'd said, as he climbed into the front seat of the Range Rover. 'Sorry for no chitty-chat. Er, I *zuppose* you *could* let us know if you're ever in London . . .'

He handed over a business card with his telephone number on one side. On the other, it said:

Mysterio

10, Downing Street

The car moved away, lit by the flash-flash-flash of cameras, and, as it passed Hamish, he found himself locking eyes with the Prime Minister . . . and shuddering.

There was something very creepy about the Prime Minister now.

His eyes were wide, but it was like he wasn't looking at anything.

It was like his eyes were *blank*.

Well, That
Was Weird

The next morning, Hamish woke bright and early.

Like everyone else in Starkley, he didn't really have a choice.

One nice thing about his town was that lots of people still had milk delivered in the morning. Most places don't have milk floats going door to door any more.

Even in Starkley, things were changing as some people bought their milk from Shop Til You Pop or had it delivered in a big van by the giant out-of-town supermarket, Foodface. Jimmy called it 'the relentless onslaught of commerce', but not even Jimmy knew what that meant.

But every morning, in the wee small hours, tiny Margarine Crinkle would clamber into her battered electric milk float and pootle it right the way through Starkley, stopping to deliver glass bottles of milk on every street, like a sort of calcium fairy.

It sounds magical, doesn't it? Such an old-fashioned and

wonderful way of life! So simple, and so lovely! One woman, against the elements, early in the morning, delivering bottles!

In fact, it was really annoying.

Margarine Crinkle was about ninety-five years old and she was a terrible driver. Just the worst.

Every morning at 5 a.m., the people of Starkley would be jolted from their sleep by the sound of her milk float hitting a lamp post, or knocking off the wing mirrors of all the parked cars on the street and setting off their alarms.

SCREEEEEECH.

Ker-KLATTER-thunk-thunk.

BEEEEEP BEEEEEP BEEEEEP.

Then they'd hear her yelling some really *terrible* words indeed as she stumbled out of the milk float – which had probably crashed into someone's hedge by now or might even be rolling down a hill because she hadn't put the brake on.

Also, her knees hurt. And her ankles. And she was having awful trouble with her wrists. And she'd shout and grumble about these ailments all the way up your garden path and back down again.

And, as they lay there in their beds, eyes wide open, every

person on the street would silently count the number of bottles they could hear Margarine Crinkle drop as she walked to their doorstep.

She was the LOUDEST milk lady anyone had ever come across. But, because she was also the last of her kind, everyone knew it was important to let her just carry on.

Hamish stared at the ceiling, thinking about the Prime Minister and trying very hard to concentrate on—

CLATTER!

Ahem. On exactly what could have happened to have made him go all—

CRASH! TINKLE! SMASH!

On precisely what could have—

BEEP! BEEP! VEHICLE REVERSING! VEHICLE REVERSING!

On the exact reasons that—

'OH, NO! ME VAN'S OFF! COME BACK! COME BACK! OOF! ME POOR OLD KNEES!'

Maybe it was just time to get up.

'Well, that was weird,' said Alice, taking off her coat and walking into Hamish's house. 'Everyone's saying it.'

She held up a copy of the *Starkley Post*.

There was a picture of the Prime Minister in his little blue pants and the headline:

<u>WELL, THAT WAS WEIRD</u>

'I really don't think anyone expected the Prime Minister to start showing everyone his pants,' said Alice. 'Mum says he's probably been under a lot of pressure because he was working so hard, but then Dad said that couldn't be true because he's a politician.'

'Maybe it's normal,' said Hamish, shrugging. 'I've never seen *Question Me Silly* before. Maybe he always finishes it with a New Pants Dance.'

'That would mean an awful lot of new pants, Hamish. I don't think grown-ups buy new pants. I think they just wear them until they dissolve in puddles of grown-up sweat. Anyway, the Prime Minister is back in London now, and you know what that means.'

Hamish looked puzzled. What did that mean?

'It means we've got to go there!' said Alice. 'You can't *nearly* meet the Prime Minister and then *not* meet him! So I've been looking at bus timetables.'

She pulled out a list of bus times so long it unfurled all the way to her feet.

Well, thought Hamish, *the strange Belgian man in the purple suit did say I should let him know if I was ever in London . . . but he didn't really mean it, did he? He was just being polite, wasn't he?*

'Now I think we should leave as quickly as possible,' said Alice, 'so that we can catch the Prime Minister before he has his tea.'

Hamish thought about it as he picked up a bag of rubbish to take out to the bins.

'I'm not really sure I'm allowed to go all the way to London on my own,' he said, opening the door. 'What with me being ten. You too for that matter.'

'My uncle could pick us up at the station,' said Alice, following him out. 'And we could eat a kebab. And you could meet the Prime Minister. And we could see the big city. And we could eat a kebab. And ride on red buses. While eating kebabs.'

'You really want a kebab, don't you?' said Hamish.

'But more importantly,' said Alice, making her most important face, 'we could go to No. 1 Arcadian Lane and see if we can work out why the blackbird wanted you to go there!'

Hamish thought about it some more as the morning sun warmed his face.

'I'd have to ask my mum,' he said.

'We could be back by the evening,' said Alice, feeling Hamish's resolve weakening. 'And you can tell her my uncle will be with us the whole time.'

But Hamish had a question for Alice. Something that had been troubling him.

'Did you notice anything . . . *strange* happening during the TV show last night?'

Alice widened her eyes.

She held up the photo of the PM in his little blue pants again.

'No – *before* the New Pants Dance,' said Hamish. 'Did you notice a slight rumble?'

'A rumble?' she said.

'A rumble and then a pop?'

'Hmm,' said Alice. 'Sounds like you had some serious tummy trouble.'

Hamish frowned. So Alice hadn't noticed the way the room seemed almost to move. Or the spotlights bursting overhead. Or the way the Prime Minister's eyes had seemed to go empty, hollow, blank . . .

The last time he'd noticed something that no one else had, the world had been in serious trouble. What if something bad was happening again? Maybe this was all linked somehow? What if this was something to do with the Neverpeople? His dad might need his help!

'What are you two talking about?' said Buster, wandering up the path with a broom. He had a part-time job clearing away all the broken milk bottles Margarine Crinkle left everywhere. It could have been a *full*-time job, to be honest. 'Is this important **PDF** business?'

'You know there's no Pause Defence Force since the world stopped stopping,' said Hamish. 'We're just kids again! All that's at an end!'

'Every end is just another beginning!' said Alice, who seemed to like that phrase almost as much as 'be prepared'.

'Who wants to be just kids again?' said Buster, sadly, leaning on his broom. 'And anyway we can't stop being the **PDF!** What if the world needs saving again? *Someone* needs to be ready!'

'Yes!' said Alice. 'Always be prepared! Have I taught you *nothing*, by repeatedly saying the same thing over and over?'

Hamish looked at his friends, and thought about how much they'd achieved together as the **PDF**. If something strange was afoot, then they were right: someone needed to be ready.

'Let me talk to my mum,' he said, thinking that maybe – just maybe – a trip to London might not be such a bad idea after all.

5

Let's Go to London!

At the rickety bus stop in the town square by the clock, Hamish's mum was all jangly and jittery.

'Have you got everything, chicken?' she said, her nerves getting the better of her. 'Have you got your Chomps? Have you got your watch?'

Hamish checked his wrist again. There it was. The watch his dad had given him. The Explorer. It had proved extremely useful the last time things had gone crazy. And it meant the world to Hamish because it was from his dad.

'What about your helmet?' asked Mum.

'I don't think I need it.'

'You should wear a helmet on the bus!' she said. 'In case things fall on your head! And have you packed your shin pads? Have you tucked your trousers into your socks?'

Hamish nodded. His mum was always telling him to tuck his trousers into his socks on long journeys these days. She'd learned that 'advice' from Hamish's

40

permanently-terrified friend Robin.

Nowadays, she worried about a lot of silly things.

– That Hamish might get in trouble with the police.

– That Hamish might go on a boat without a life jacket.

– That Hamish might sit on a shopping trolley and
accidentally barrel down a big hill.

Hamish gave his mum a reassuring pat on the arm. Since
his dad had vanished, Hamish and Jimmy had become extra
precious to Mum. Hamish understood why because she had
become extra precious to him too.

'I can't believe I'm letting you do this,' she said, shaking her
head and folding her arms. 'London can be very unfriendly!
And are you sure the Prime Minister's people said it was all
right?'

'Well . . .' began Hamish.

'Yes!' said Alice. 'Mysterio gave Hamish a card and said,
"PLEASE COME!" Clear as day! Except for the accent.'

'Well, it's only because I trust you,' said Hamish's mum.
'And Alice, your uncle will be there to pick you both up and
take you straight to the Prime Minister?'

'Yes, Mrs Ellerby,' said Alice, using her responsible voice.
'Uncle Peter is really very trustworthy. He's a policeman.
And I've packed an extra baguette for Hamish.'

The 10.11 coach to London pulled into view.

'We'll be there by lunchtime,' said Alice. 'Honestly, Mrs Ellerby, I do this all the time. It's not like we're going to some whole other world!'

'So you do this all the time?' said Hamish, as the coach whizzed through the countryside.

'No, this is the first,' said Alice, looking out of the window. 'I've never been to London before. But sometimes you have to treat adults with kid gloves.'

'How long has your Uncle Peter been a policeman?' he asked.

'Oh, you know. A while or so. Anyway, I can't believe your mum makes you tuck your socks into your trousers.'

'Robin's mum told her that it reduces the chance of unnecessary trippage,' said Hamish and Alice laughed. She'd *never* do that.

Hamish was a little nervous to be away from home without his mum, so he concentrated on what lay ahead. Alice seemed pretty sure that all they had to do was turn up at Downing Street and the Prime Minister would welcome them with open arms.

And of course there was one other thing to do. Hamish

hadn't mentioned it to his mum because he didn't want to worry her. But he planned to take a detour to Arcadian Lane. He wondered what it could be. Maybe it was a huge skyscraper. Or a grand old house. Perhaps it was a museum. Or a video-games arcade. Maybe his dad would be there. Or maybe all this was for nothing at all.

Now that Hamish knew his dad was out there somewhere (and that there was a reason he'd gone) he missed him more than ever. He thought that going to Arcadian Lane would make him feel like he was closer to his dad, somehow.

Alice got a baguette out as the driver switched on the coach TV.

Life's a Dream with Vapidia Sheen was on.

Hamish sighed. Not this again. It was always on. So many people watched it, even though none of them could really put their finger on why. Hamish thought people watched it just because it was on so often.

Vapidia was a big star. She had jet-black, glossy hair and was the first-ever winner of that singing show, *Spin Me Round*.

Have you seen *Spin Me Round*? People have to sing while someone spins them round. It's a very clever format.

People had liked Vapidia because she could sing really well, no matter what direction she was facing. And she was bright and loud. She'd studied rocket science at university and could count up to a trillion. But then she got her own show and her personality seemed to change overnight. Now she just walked around, saying weird things.

Things like 'I really like coasters' and then pointing at a coaster.

Or 'Look at this wall' and then pointing at a wall.

Here is how the TV section of the *Starkley Post* describes *Life's a Dream with Vapidia Sheen*.

Life's a Dream with Vapidia Sheen

Episode 17:

Vapidia sees a lamp post and reads a bit of paper.

Episode 25:

Vapidia has a nap for a bit.

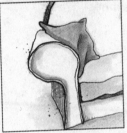

Episode 48:

Vapidia thinks she hears a distant aeroplane.

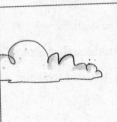

Episode 102:

Vapidia changes the ink in her printer and then has another quick nap.

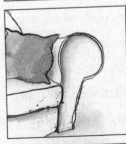

Episode 194:

Vapidia drops a spoon in a cafe (but they didn't film that bit).

MADA

COU

COU

INTERNATIONAL WO

THIS WEEK'S
SWEETS OF T.

LORD OF TI

Come to Lord
for Chips! Ch
Chips! Chips! C
Chips! Chip
CHIPS! CHII
And battered

Slackjaw's

Yeuch! Dullsville. Boretown. Tedium City. Blandling, Ohio.

Who'd watch *that*?

Well, plenty of people actually. Most of Starkley, night after night. It was the most popular show in the whole country. And no one but Hamish seemed to notice that Vapidia's big brown eyes just seemed . . . empty.

No, not empty. What's the word?

They seemed *blank*.

Alice suddenly nudged him.

'Look!' she said, excited.

They were arriving in London!

Pressed up against their window, they took it all in.

The skyscrapers of Canary Wharf. The building that looks like a gherkin. The grand old BT Tower in the distance, rising above it all.

'And look! The **Cutty Sark!'** said Alice, catching a glimpse of the very old ship with its huge sails as they drove alongside the river. 'And there's a sign for the Observatory!'

Hamish had always wanted to go to the Royal Observatory. He loved the idea of telescopes. He'd asked his brother for a telescope for Christmas. He knew exactly the one he wanted. A **Gia-tron BugEye 5000** in British Racing

Green. It was a right old stunner. But Jimmy had just said, 'What do you need a telescope for when you can just stand closer to stuff?'

Hamish didn't feel nervous to be out of Starkley any more. He felt excited. He would see the Prime Minister. And then he would find Arcadian Lane.

'Next stop,' called out the driver over the tannoy, 'Victoria Station!'

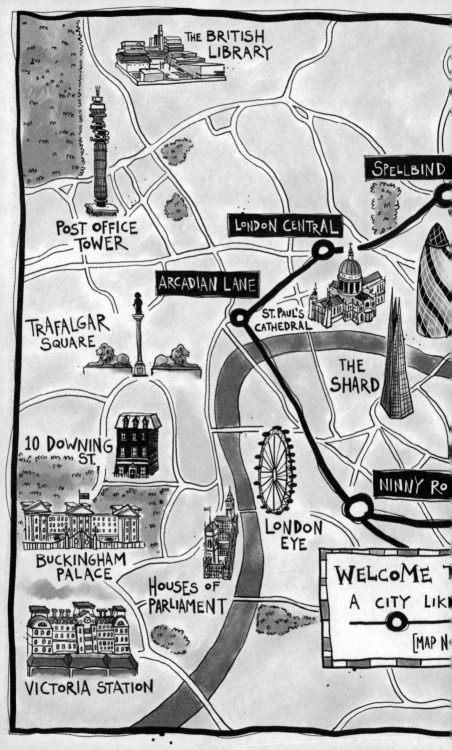

Taxi!

This place was insane!

What. The. Heck?!

Hamish had never *seen* so many people.

People of all sizes, wearing all sorts of clothes, from all over the world, poured out of huge, noisy coaches. Black fumes poured out from behind them.

From behind the coaches I mean – not from behind the people. If black fumes poured out of the *people's* behinds, they should really see a doctor.

There were coaches from Scotland. Coaches from Wales. Coaches that had driven all the way from Spain and Germany and France. They all had different names written on the side.

A green and brown coach with

REG'S GUERNSEY FUN BUS!

scrawled along it.

A sleek yellow and blue one marked

GLOBALFLØBAL OF SWEDEN.

50

'I'll take you on the scenic route,' said Leo, putting the taxi into reverse, mounting the pavement and knocking over a bin. 'No extra charge!'

Leo certainly gave them the scenic route. The little satnav on his dashboard kept trying to tell him which way to go and he kept hitting it and muttering.

They saw the London Eye.

St Paul's Cathedral.

They passed Buckingham Palace, where they saw men in bearskin hats twirling their guns and stamping their feet.

They sped down Horse Guards Parade, and spotted soldiers on horseback, waving bright, shiny swords.

At Piccadilly Circus, dozens of teenage boys stared up

And a German one just called **FAHRT**.

A man carrying a tuba tried to inch his way past a group of Swiss girls wearing backpacks the size of small cars.

"Scuse me!' he shouted, rudely. **'SCUSE ME!'**

Everyone seemed in quite a hurry to see London, which was weird because it's not like it was going to disappear. **'OUT OF THE WAY!'** yelled a red-faced woman with a tiny suitcase under her arm, and Hamish jumped. People weren't like this in Starkley.

Hamish stood a little sheepishly by a bench while Alice studied a giant map behind him. Standing by a bench had always made him feel safe. It's because benches, like London, don't go anywhere. And, if you stand by a bench, well – you're not going anywhere either.

Yet another huge coach arrived and dozens more people leapt out to fetch suitcases and bags. It made Hamish feel tiny. And then he realised he couldn't see Alice any more.

'Alice!' he shouted. 'Alice?'

Where had she gone? Hamish put his hand on the bench for reassurance.

Oh, brilliant, he thought. *Alice has been kidnapped.* That just showed how rude people in London could be! Or she'd gone off without him. Or she'd ended up in some sewers. Hamish's

mum had been right to worry.

Hamish suddenly wished he'd brought a helmet.

Well, at least he was still at the coach station. He could just wait for the next bus back to Starkley and get straight on it. At least he could say he'd *been* to London, even if it was just the coach station. But what about Downing Street? What about Arcadian Lane?

And then . . .

'Oy–OY!' someone shouted, cheerfully. 'Oy–OY!'

A tubby man was leaning from the window of a luminous green London taxi. The kind of green no one in their right mind would ever paint *anything*. All the other taxis were black – but not this one.

'You called Hamish?' shouted the man, who had enormous glasses, a big nose, a squat body and a thick thatch of hair bursting out of his ears.

'Y-yes?' said Hamish, uncertainly.

'Got a mate of yours in the back!' he said, and he sounded his horn twice, for effect. 'Oy–OY!'

The back window rolled down to reveal Alice.

'Come on, H,' she said. 'Hop in!'

'I thought your uncle was picking us up,' said Hamish,

bouncing round the cab as it roared off down Buckir Palace Road.

'Oh . . . yes,' said Alice, hanging on to the hand grips. been delayed.'

'So where's the first stop?' asked the driver, pushing glasses up and turning his radio down.

'Number ten Downing Street,' said Alice. 'It's the Prir Minister's house. Do you know it?'

'Oh, yeah, I've heard of it,' said the driver, whose identit badge read **LEOPOLD BANNISTER**.

'Why is your taxi so green?' asked Alice, and Hamish fe embarrassed.

'Why shouldn't it be green?' said Leo. 'You can't just do th same as everybody else in life! You gotta stand out! yourself! What's the point of just blending in?'

Hamish could hear the radio. Someone was talking the Prime Minister's New Pants Dance and w showing your undies on live TV meant you shouldr be Prime Minister any more . . .

'Oh, *rats*,' said Leo, suddenly jamming on the br

They'd hit a traffic jam. Hamish could see n cars, one after the other, right the way to the street, all of them angrily beeping their horns.

blankly at a giant poster of Vapidia Sheen.

'Saddos,' said Alice.

But it was exciting to see all these famous buildings and places!

Soon they were at Trafalgar Square, where the big stone lions lay beneath the statue of Lord Nelson, and, in the distance, Hamish noticed a police van pulling up and bundling someone into the back. He'd never seen action like this in Starkley! Well, not since all the monsters left.

'Oy—OY!' yelled Leo. 'So how come you two are in London all alone?'

'We're not really,' said Hamish. 'Alice's Uncle Peter lives here, except he's a bit busy being a policeman.'

'Oh, yeah?' said Leo. 'Where's Uncle Peter live?'

'Um,' said Alice, looking at the ceiling of the cab. 'In an area called . . . Shaddington.'

'Shaddington?'

'Yes. Um, No. 4 Parsley Grove.'

'*Parsley Grove?*' said Leo, frowning. 'I don't know that one. What police station does he work at?'

'Er . . . the main one?' said Alice.

Hamish looked at her, suspiciously.

'Oh, *rats!*' said Leo once more, as they hit a right and pulled up at Downing Street.

Because there were people. *Everywhere.*

Some of the crowd held placards saying '**WE DON'T WANT TO SEE YOUR PANTS!**' and chanted, as nervous-looking police officers held them back. Reporters from all over the country had set up TV cameras outside the famous black front door. A helicopter circled overhead, and more people arrived with signs saying things like '*YOU'RE PANTS!*' and '**PANTSGATE!**' and '**WE WANT PANTSWERS! (answers)**'.

It was *impossible* to get to the door. It seemed people wanted the Prime Minister to come out and explain himself and weren't going to budge until he did.

'Looks like you ain't going to Downing Street today, kids,'

said Leo, sadly. 'Anyway, that's eleven pounds fifty.'

'But it's *important*,' said Alice, staring out of the window at the crowds. 'It's important we get there!'

'Important?' said Leo.

'*Vital*,' she said. 'We were invited. By the Prime Minister's assistant.'

'Was you now?' said Leo, impressed. 'What, that Canadian fella?'

'Yes,' said Alice. 'Because my friend Hamish Ellerby here saved the world. Well, we both did. And the Prime Minister has made it *very* clear he wants to meet Hamish.'

'Saved the world?' said Leo. 'Yeah, I heard something about that on the radio.'

'There wouldn't *be* a radio if it wasn't for Hamish,' said Alice. 'Or a Big Ben, or tennis balls, or films, or snot, or a rubber industry, or luminous green taxi cabs taking scenic routes through London just so they can charge kids extra!'

Leo looked embarrassed. He'd been caught out. He thought about what Alice had said.

'Well, if it's that important . . .' he said, with a grin, 'I *do* know a back way . . .'

Ten Frowning Street

Do you know how long it takes to be a taxi driver in London?

'It takes forever!' said Leo, screeching round a corner at full speed. 'My grandson put this computer box thingy in the car that's always trying to tell me what to do! He thought it'd save me time, but it just winds me up!'

'Go straight ahead,' said the little satnav on his dashboard in a very posh voice.

'I KNOW!' shouted Leo. 'I KNOW THE WAY!'

He kept trying to talk to it like it could hear him.

'Go straight ahead,' it said again, politely. 'To that roundabout over there.'

'I KNOW!' shouted Leo, going quite red. 'WHY ARE YOU TELLING ME THIS?'

Hamish and Alice glanced at each other as they came to a roundabout. Did this madman really know a back way into Downing Street?

'*Continue round the roundabout,*' said the satnav, as Leo sighed.

'Thing is, we train to be taxi drivers for years!' said Leo.

'*Continue round the roundabout,*' said the satnav.

'We have to learn every little nook and cranny of the city!' he said.

'*Continue round the roundabout,*' said the satnav.

'We have to know every side street, every bump in the road!'

'*Continue round the roundabout,*' said the satnav.

Alice nudged Hamish. They'd been going round and round this roundabout for ages. They'd just been going round in circles while Leo complained! The same statues kept passing by outside the window!

'People think we can be replaced by robots!' said Leo, shaking his head, lost in his thoughts. 'It's robots that'll get us in the end!'

'*Continue round the roundabout,*' said the satnav.

'We've been going in circles for ages,' said Hamish. 'Maybe we should . . .'

'I KNOW!' yelled Leo. 'I KNOW WHAT I'M DOING!'

Moments later, on a road called The Mall, Leo took a sneaky left.

'Horse Guards Road,' he whispered. 'Right, you two – get down. And don't worry – like every cabbie, I've passed my Gift of the Gab test.'

Hamish and Alice hid on the floor of the taxi. Gift of the Gab test? What was Leo up to? And then the car squeaked to a halt.

'Oy–OY! officer!' said Leo, and Hamish's eyes widened. Leo was talking to a policeman! His mum had been right! He was going to get arrested!

'No taxis down this way today, please, sir,' said the policeman. 'This is a restricted area. Turn around now, please.'

'But I am on a secret mission, officer,' said Leo, and then he picked up a small packet of mints. 'I'm bringing the PM his mints.'

'His . . . mints?' said the policeman, eyeing Leo with great suspicion.

'His mints, sir. Haven't you seen what's going on round the front? It's not like he can pop out to the shops himself!'

'Here – you've eaten half of these,' said the officer, studying the packet.

Leo shrugged.

'Did you see him on telly last night? He's not himself lately. That's precisely what the Prime Minister asked for – half a packet of mints delivered in a bright green cab.'

The policeman looked unsure.

'This seems most irregular.'

'Well, I wouldn't question it if I was you,' said Leo. 'He's in a foul mood today because no one liked his pants.'

The policeman considered all this.

'All right,' he said. 'But be quick about it!'

Leo drove on, round the corner, until they came to a small patch of grass with a statue of a man called Mountbatten on it.

'See those hedges over there?' said Leo. 'There's a wall behind them. You get over that and you're in the Prime Minister's back garden . . . but you'll need to be quick. You can't be spotted!'

'Thank you, Leo,' said Hamish.

'Here's my number,' said Leo, handing them a small green business card. 'This trip's on me, on account of the whole, er, "scenic route" thing. If you need me, just call!'

And so Alice and Hamish got out of the taxi, and ran as fast as they could towards the Prime Minister's hedges before anyone saw them.

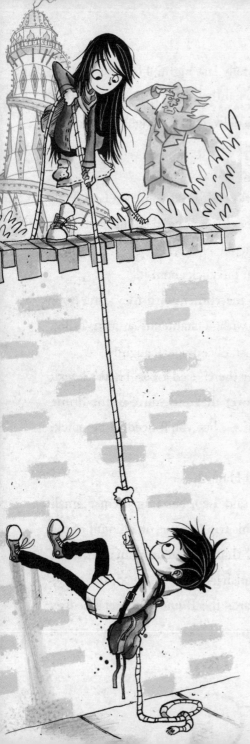

Alice scaled the wall first and dropped down a short rope she'd pulled from her bag.

'You brought a rope?' said Hamish, as he climbed up it.

'ALWAYS BE PREPARED!'

she yelled.

They jumped down together.

There were huge trees in the Prime Minister's back garden.

A hot tub.

A barbeque.

An outdoor bowling alley.

A zip wire.

A pizza oven.

A miniature adventure playground.

Swingball. Ping-pong. Minigolf. A huge piñata shaped like a hedgehog.

A swimming pool with a massive helter-skelter slide.

It was *amazing*.

Well, except for the weird, giant golden statue of the Prime Minister staring at a pen, which he'd had made to celebrate the day he thought he'd fixed one with his mind.

'This place has everything,' said Hamish, checking out the skate ramp.

'I HAVE JUST ONE THING TO SAY TO YOU!' bellowed a voice from somewhere behind them. They spun round and immediately lost all courage. Caught!

'Oh!' said Hamish, panicking. 'I'm so s-s-sorry! We'll go!'

In front of them was a very tall man in military uniform. He was wearing a beret and shiny black boots and was standing to attention with his hands behind his back. Hamish thought he'd seen this guy on TV.

No, wait – he'd been in Starkley, when they'd rushed the PM away! That's where Hamish had seen him!

'AND THAT ONE THING,' he said, very loudly, and quite angrily, **'IS AS FOLLOWS . . .'**

Hamish wanted to cry. He hated being in trouble. And now he was going to be told off by a grown-up. And not just any grown-up. A grown-up in a uniform! They're the very *worst* types of grown-up to be told off by!

Both Alice and Hamish squinted and squirmed as they waited for the man to say the one thing he wanted to say. Oh, this was going to be bad. He had leaned right down and was pausing for effect. That meant he was going to *really* tell them off.

Which is when the man took a deep breath and said . . .

'If I had a cat, I'd call him Poopy.'

The kids stayed quiet for a moment. Alice glanced at Hamish and then back at the man.

Hamish didn't really understand either. He wanted to clarify.

'Sorry, did you—'

'I SAID THE ONE THING I WANT TO SAY RIGHT NOW IS THAT IF I HAD A CAT I'D CALL HIM POOPY!' yelled the man, with his face now just centimetres from Hamish. **'OR MAYBE *MR POOPY*, I'M NOT SURE!'**

And, as Hamish looked properly for the first time into the man's eyes, he shuddered.

He had the same blank look that the Prime Minister had in the car as he left Starkley. It was like he wasn't really there.

Behind him, the back doors of Downing Street were flung open.

'SERGEANT MAJOR, STOP RUNNIN' AWAY!' shouted Mysterio, flustered. **'COME BACK IN HEEYAR AT WANCE!'**

Now that the doors were open, there was a lot of shouting coming out of 10 Downing Street. Hamish could hear glass smashing and things being knocked over and Mysterio seemed very keen to get back in.

He stopped in his tracks when he saw a confused Hamish Ellerby and Alice Shepherd standing right there in the back garden, when he was pretty sure they should have been in Starkley.

'And I zappose **YOU** better come insidey as well . . .' he whispered.

The Prime
Minister's Diary

Inside 10 Downing Street it was utter mayhem.

Turkish rugs were all squiffy. Velvet drapes had fallen from their rails. A cat chased a dog up the bannisters. There was a lot of shouting. And it seemed like anything that could have been knocked over had been knocked over.

'You betta come upstairs,' said Mysterio, sadly. 'You's not gonna **BELIEF** your eyes.'

Up the polished wooden stairs, all the grand paintings of old Prime Ministers were wonky.

There was the portrait of Prime Minister Englebert Fetch and his unusually curled moustache.

There was Monika Potts, holding her *Prime Minister of the Year* Award (she was the only person who could have won, to be fair).

There was Jobb Dunn, looking very serious and giving two thumbs ups, even though he never actually did anything.

There was Alistair Plumb with his monocle and very unusual socks.

And there was Tabatha Gurnley, just eating a sausage and smiling, like she always did.

'I can't believe we're actually here,' said Hamish, amazed.

But the smile soon faded as Mysterio pushed open the huge oak doors of the Prime Minister's Office and they saw what was inside.

All the important people that Hamish and Alice usually saw on television were behaving very oddly indeed.

The Prime Minister had a cat on his head.

The Minister of Defence was just spinning around in her chair.

The Chancellor of the Exchequer was doing squat thrusts on the table.

And the noise!

Everyone was talking at once.

'I GOT A BOO-BOO!' the Minister of Defence kept shouting, as she spun round.

'Has anybody seen my knees?' asked the Health Minister. 'Has anybody seen my knees?'

'Who wants to look at my pants again?' yelled the Prime Minister, proudly, from in front of a large portrait of him

lifting sixteen cans of Fanta.

Hamish and Alice stood in shocked silence. This was definitely *not* what they were expecting from the people in charge of the country.

Suddenly, they had to jump out of the way as Mayor Bunkum rode through the room on a bicycle, ringing his bell and holding his bike helmet.

'Sorry!' he said, as he knocked a priceless vase from its perch and rode on, bumping down the stairs. 'Sorry!'

'Even the *Mayor's* like this!' said Alice, in disbelief.

'He's alwayz like that, to be honest,' said Mysterio, quietly.

'What's happened to them all?' said Hamish. 'How did they get this way?'

'We gotta Prime Minister home last night,' said Mysterio. 'And we just was *finding* everybody like thees!'

'IF I HAD A CAT, I'D CALL HIM POOPY!' shouted the Sergeant Major, right into Mysterio's ear.

'I GOT A BOO-BOO!' yelled the Minister of Defence.

'Alice,' said Hamish, quietly. 'Have you noticed their eyes?'

Each and every set of eyes was large and round and *blank*.

Alice pulled Hamish to one side.

'Hamish,' she whispered. 'Do you think *this* is what "Neverpeople" are?'

Hamish thought about that for a moment. 'The name doesn't make sense,' he said. 'Because these *were* people. I mean, they still *are* people. But something's happened to them for sure. The same thing that happened to the Prime Minister in Starkley last night.'

Alice put her hands on her hips. 'Well, who's running the country now?' she said. 'I mean, there are things to be done. They have to make speeches and squabble. They can't just say "I want a cat called Poopy" or "Where are my knees?" all day. They have to decide on important stuff like how much Chomps cost or where you can park your bike.'

She was right. The country was in peril. Who knew *how* much Chomps would cost from now on? And, in that moment, Hamish realised he had been right to trust his instincts. He'd known something wasn't right the second it had happened to the Prime Minister. He'd known it as he stared into his eyes. He should have done something there and then and then maybe this wouldn't have happened to the rest of them.

Well, he wouldn't be making that mistake again.

He walked over to the Prime Minister's desk as Mayor Bunkum rode back through on his bike, knocking a set of expensive-looking dishes off a sideboard with a **CLATTER**

and an **OOPS!** Mysterio chased after him, yelling
'PRESS THE BRAKES! PRESS THE BRAAAAKES!'

'Hamish,' said Alice, in the middle of all the confusion, 'I don't like this. Maybe you were right before and it was a mistake to come to London. Maybe we should just go home to Starkley. We've got Leo's number . . .'

'Good idea, Alice,' he replied, picking up the bright red telephone on the PM's desk. 'We'll call him.'

'And ask him to take us back to the station?'

'No,' said Hamish, picking up the Prime Minister's diary and studying it.

'What?' said Alice. 'Ask him to take us all the way back to Starkley? He'd definitely need his satnav for that!'

'No,' said Hamish again, now looking very pale indeed because he had spotted something incredible.

'Where then?' said Alice. 'Hamish? What's wrong?'

Hamish held up the Prime Minister's diary, and pointed at today's date.

Underneath it, in the fancy handwriting that Hamish recognised from his letter, the Prime Minister had written:

Important Meeting, 2 p.m.
1 Arcadian Lane.

The Prime Minister was supposed to be going to a meeting at the very place Hamish and Alice were intending to go! The very place the blackbird had shown them!

Hamish checked The Explorer. It was 1.30 p.m.

Alice's eyes widened as she took it all in.

Imagine how wide they'd have gone if she'd known that it wasn't just the country that was in peril . . . but the whole world.

9

Careful!

I'd better tell you right here and now.

The bit I was warning you about is coming up in a minute.

The bit I said would blow your mind.

The Big Secret.

Are you ready? Can you cope? Because I'll say it one last time: this is your last chance to put the book down before everything you think you know is turned on its head, all at once.

No? OK. But don't say I didn't warn you . . .

▶◀

Alice and Hamish were in the back of Leo's taxi, and Leo was confused.

'Oy–OY!' Arcadian Lane?' he said. 'What you wanna go there for? I ain't been there in years!'

'Look, Alice,' said Hamish, pointing out of the window. 'Do you notice anything?'

Alice looked around, but couldn't tell what Hamish meant.

There were so many buildings and people. Some poured out of department stores like John Lewis, or shops like Miss Selfridge. Others stood in queues in Burger King, or next to vans selling Mr Whippy ice creams.

'Look closer,' said Hamish. 'The posters!'

They were passing a giant billboard of Vapidia Sheen. People were taking selfies in front of it, their huge, wide eyes staring blankly.

The more Hamish looked, the more blank people he could see.

Models on posters. Blank.

The weatherman on the TV in the shop window. Blank.

At some traffic lights, the driver of a big red bus turned to look at Hamish.

Hamish shuddered. The man's eyes were blank!

Yet no one else seemed to notice. Normal people were milling around, staring at their phones as they walked, oblivious.

'Something's definitely going on,' said Hamish. He was worried.

Ʞ

The cab pulled into a side street and slowed to a halt.

So this was No. 1 Arcadian Lane.

A grand old red-tiled building that had seen better days. *Many* better days. One great big shutter down the middle. Boarded-up windows on each side. Old, tattered posters, faded and ripped on each one. A round blue and red sign above it all, dusty and browned.

'It used to be a tube station,' said Leo, leaning out of the window of his cab, as the kids got out and stared. 'You know – the underground railway.'

'But it isn't any more?' asked Hamish, his heart sinking.

This couldn't be it, could it? An old, disused underground station? He dusted off some dirt from the wall. A big black 'I' was revealed.

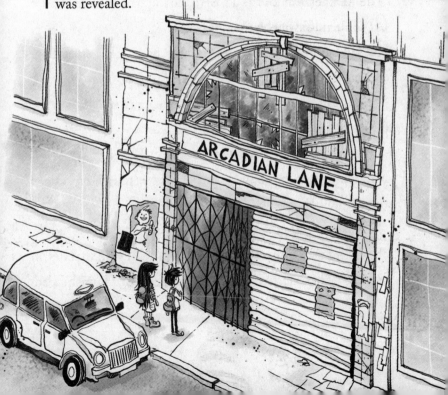

'Hasn't been used in years,' said Leo. 'They call 'em Ghost Stations. They're all over London. They were shut down over the years. Yeah, let me think – there's Arcadian Lane, Dog Walk, The Ship . . . about ten of 'em.'

Hamish looked around. There was no one else about. He checked his watch. It was nearly 2 p.m.

'Thanks for bringing us, Leo,' said Hamish.

'You gonna be all right here?' he said, sensing Hamish was saying he could go. 'You sure you don't want me to take you back to Victoria?'

'We'll be okay from here,' said Alice.

'You got my number!' said Leo, moving the cab off. 'Oy– OY!' The kids watched him leave.

'A Ghost Station?' asked Alice. 'I have, like, six billion questions right now.'

They heard the sound of Big Ben striking two o'clock in the distance.

Which is when they felt a breeze.

'And I will do my best to answer those questions,' said a voice from behind them.

Hamish and Alice spun round.

Standing right there was the woman they'd seen that day in Starkley. The one that had told them about Hamish's dad.

76

She'd said that he was a hero, which had filled Hamish with hope and made him feel better about not having his dad around. She was dressed in white, and on her lapel was a badge with a logo Hamish recognised – a sunflower with wings.

Belasko. The company his dad was supposed to work for.

'I'll be honest,' said the woman, 'I was expecting to brief the Prime Minister. Not two ten-year-olds. But I had a feeling you'd come here eventually . . .'

'How?' asked Hamish.

'Because you remind me of someone,' said the woman. 'Someone else who turned up recently . . .'

'Someone from Starkley?' asked Hamish.

'Oh, no,' she said. 'Someone a *world away* from Starkley.'

'Yes, well, I'm sorry it's just us two ten-year-olds,' said Alice. 'But the Prime Minister is a little busy with his pants right now.'

'Then it's true,' said the woman, frowning. 'They got to him.'

'Who?' asked Hamish. 'The Neverpeople? Is *that* who's doing all this?'

'Exactly the opposite,' she said, with a gentle smile. 'It's time.'

Hamish and Alice looked at each other.

'Time for what?' asked Hamish.

'Time you knew,' she said.

WELCOME TO BELASKO!

Be Vigilant. Stay Vigilant!

Hello, recruit – and welcome
to the hidden world of Belasko.

**Did you know Belasko is a Basque word
meaning raven? Well, it is!**

For thousands of years, black birds
have been linked to magic. Mystery.
Secrets. The Unknown.

The purpose of Belasko is to know
the unknown. We are the Vigilant.

Our past glories are many!

Who could forget the epic battle
against B.E.A.S.T. and The Shrinkers?
Who doesn't remember the war
on Intelli-vile?
Who shudders not, as they recall
The Great Stink?

We must fight those who would
do the world harm!

Now say this loud and proud:

Before there was the Before.
Now there is the Now.
After there will be the After.
And then there will be the Then.

I pledge allegiance to the Vigilant.
I pledge allegiance to Belasko.
I will do right, not wrong.
I will always be prepared.

Signed, in secret,

Hamish Ellerby.   *Alice Shepherd*

On behalf of the Starkley PDF

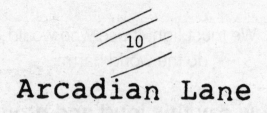

10

Arcadian Lane

The woman in white flung open the door of No. 1 Arcadian Lane.

'Thank you for signing that,' she said, slightly out of breath. 'Sorry to be a bore, but we have to maintain a certain level of secrecy.'

But Hamish and Alice weren't listening. They were staring. Because this place was magnificent.

You would never have guessed it looked like this from the outside. Or that there was this *much* of it.

It was huge, with a curved ceiling that seemed to disappear into the horizon, lit by thousands of bright white lights.

The floor tiles were white too, and there was a giant clock above it all, surrounded by stained glass. The sun streamed through it, making everything even brighter and more colourful.

'It's like a spaceship!' said Hamish.

There were beautiful bright blue tiles on the wall, spelling

out Arcadian Lane, but, even though this place looked a bit
like it was from the future, all the adverts on the walls were
really old and faded.

'I'm afraid what you will see today may well cause you
never to sleep again,' said the lady. 'First, though, we need to
get in here.'

She pointed at a very normal-looking passport photo
machine.

'Why?' said Alice. 'Do we need ID? I've got my leisure-
centre card.'

'You'll see,' said the woman.

The three of them squeezed into the booth, which was
rather a snug fit, and the woman pulled out a silver coin.
She put it in the machine and hit the big red button.

A countdown started on the screen in front of them.

3...

2...

'Are we supposed to smile?' asked Hamish.

1...

Hamish panicked and did a really weird smile.

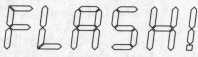

'Right. Everybody out,' said the woman. She hurried from the machine with Alice and Hamish just behind her, and strode off, trailing her hand along the tiled wall, which read:

TO THE TRAINS ⇒⇒ ⟶

Weren't they even going to wait for the photos? Hamish and Alice glanced at each other and shrugged.

As they jogged after her, Hamish caught sight of the old posters again. He had to do a double take as he ran.

Mrs? He was *sure* it had said *Mr Gibson* a moment ago.

'Where are we going?' shouted Alice, as the woman turned another corner and walked down a narrow corridor.

'You'll see!' shouted the woman, and Alice frowned.

'Ol' whatserface is a very frustrating woman,' she said, shaking her head. 'Every time you ask her something, she just says "you'll see" or "all will be revealed!"'

The two kids could feel a strange breeze now, rising and falling.

'I mean, do you think this is what she's *always* like?' continued Alice. 'If she's at the supermarket and they ask her if she's got a loyalty card, does she just say, "Ooh, time will tell!" and look all mysterious?'

The breeze was getting stronger now and blowing their hair all over the place. They could hear the rumble and squeal of an approaching train.

'Let's not miss it,' said the woman, without looking back.

'I thought these stations weren't used any more?' Hamish said. 'I thought these were – what do you call them – "Ghost Stations"?'

As the rumble grew louder, they began to run, passing more old posters for ancient-looking films and books.

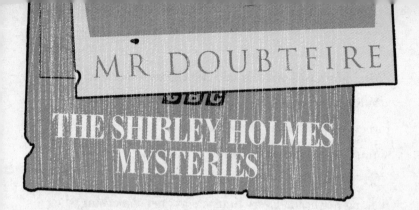

'Come on!' shouted the woman, who'd reached the platform. 'It's arriving!'

They got to her just as a huge red train **THUNDERED** into Arcadian Lane. The noise was deafening as it *SCREEEEEEECHED* and slowed. Sparks flew from underneath it and the lights above them flickered. Steam poured from the rails as it juddered to a halt with a sort of *KA-JEEEEEESSSHHHH*.

Hamish had never seen a train like this before. It looked both old-fashioned and modern.

'Where are we going?' he asked, as the woman stepped on to the train. 'And, by the way, what's your name?'

Two carriage doors slid open with a *BEEP - BEEP - BEEP*.

'Call me Alex,' said the woman, as she stepped on board.

Hamish and Alice looked at each other, uncertainly.

'What do you think?' said Hamish.

'I'm . . . not sure,' said Alice.

'Come on,' said Alex.

The train doors started to *BEEP - BEEP - BEEP* again.

'What I'm about to show you concerns the very future of life on Earth,' said Alex. 'I intended to show the Prime Minister today and get him to take action, but it looks like those plans have changed.'

Hamish didn't know what to do. He was a little scared.

'It will explain what happened to your dad, Hamish,' said Alex.

The train doors started to close. Hamish hesitated.

'It's now or never!' said Alice, grabbing his hand as she leapt aboard and pulling him on to the train just as the doors snapped shut behind him.

The train started to vibrate as the engines started up. They grew louder and louder still. The windows began to rattle and shake. It was *exactly* the way it feels when you're sitting in a plane that's about to take off.

'Hang on to something!' yelled Alex, as the train got **LOUDER** and **LOUDER** and **LOUDER** . . . 'We're about to go through The Gap!'

More sparks flew, outside the window . . .

More steam poured from the train . . .

Hamish's teeth began to chatter with the vibrations . . .

The two kids grabbed a pole as Alex shouted, 'Get ready . . .
Mind The Gap!'

BOOM!

The train SHOT OFF into the tunnel like a bullet from a gun.

All Aboard!

The train was whistling through The Gap at what felt like a million miles an hour. On a map above the seats, Hamish could see they were travelling on the **Unorthodox Line**.

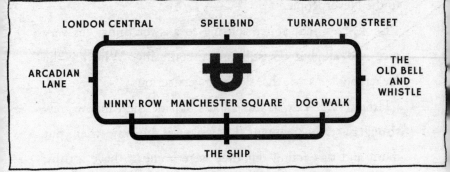

LONDON CENTRAL   SPELLBIND   TURNAROUND STREET

ARCADIAN
LANE

THE
OLD BELL
AND
WHISTLE

NINNY ROW   MANCHESTER SQUARE   DOG WALK

THE SHIP

Lights flashed by outside the windows . . . blue . . . red . . . green . . . all the colours of the rainbow. It was like they were twisting, turning, going upside down.

'This feels weird,' said Hamish, urgently. 'I told my mum we were going to Downing Street and then coming straight home.'

'We're going to a very special place,' said Alex. 'A place

which is a lot like the world you know. But very different too.'

'Belgium?' asked Alice.

'You'll see,' said Alex, smiling.

'Look, will you **JUST ANSWER A QUESTION!**' said Alice, very firmly.

'We are going to *other*London,' said Alex.

Hamish frowned. What was she on about?

'This train line is the only way to get there,' she said. 'The photo booth is the way to trigger its arrival. It's our only way to the Neverpeople.'

'Look, now that you're starting to answer things it's very nice and all, but it's still pretty confusing. Who *are* the Neverpeople?' said Alice, looking very serious.

'Hmm,' said Alex, as the colours outside the window grew stronger and more vibrant. 'Let me put it this way: when your mum and dad found out they were going to have a baby, Hamish – they didn't know you were going to be a little boy, did they?'

'Well . . . I guess not,' said Hamish, as the carriage jolted and jerked around.

'Right,' said Alex. 'And when you were in your mum's tummy they must have been thinking about what to call you, mustn't they?'

'Yes,' said Hamish. 'They said they were going to call me Hamish if I was a boy, because Dad is Scottish and Hamish is a Scottish name.'

'And what about if you were a girl?' asked Alex.

'If I was a girl?' said Hamish, looking confused, because that's a strange thought, isn't it? 'I think they said if I was a girl they were going to call me . . . *Holly*.'

'Holly?!' laughed Alice. 'Holly Ellerby? That's a lot of L's in one name. Hello, I'm Hollyellerby. Holly-ollerby. Hollyellerbelly.'

'Well, what would *you* have been called?' said Hamish, a bit defensively.

'If I'd been a boy, they would've called me Alan,' said Alice. 'A good, honest name. Trustworthy. Dependable.'

'*Alan* Shepherd?' said Hamish. 'Sounds like a driving instructor.'

'I wouldn't have minded being called Alan,' said Alice, 'And . . . *hang* on, what's this got to do with anything?'

Alex smiled.

'When someone is born in our world – their *opposite* is born elsewhere.'

Hamish and Alice looked confused.

'What?'

'*When you are born in our world, the person you* nearly *were is born in another world!*'

'So . . . wait,' said Alice. 'You're telling me that's who the Neverpeople are? Our opposites?'

'Yes,' said Alex. 'Let's say there's a girl called Jo. That means that in the other world a boy called *Joe* would be born.'

'What?!' said Alice.

'They'd have a lot in common, obviously,' said Alex. 'But also quite a lot different; they're like you, but they're not like you.'

'I think you've gone mad,' said Hamish.

'For every *he*, there's a *she*! For every Adam and Eve, there's a *Madam* and *Steve*!'

Alex looked very pleased with herself for that one.

The carriage suddenly lit up with a blinding light as they reached the end of The Gap. Hamish covered his eyes.

'We're arriving,' said Alex, as the brakes went down and sparks flew once more.

'Come on,' she said, as the doors beeped open. 'Welcome to Otherearth.'

British. Ish.

Hamish and Alice skipped up the steps of London Central Station with no idea of what they'd see next.

'Are you ready?' asked Alex, as they reached the door at the top, which had big brass shutters she was already unlocking.

Hamish could hear London on the other side. His tummy flipped slightly. Alice reached out and squeezed his hand.

Then up the shutters went and all was revealed.

London, in the sunshine, full of colour and noise.

They stepped out and looked around.

A huge sign read:

It was busy. Men and women were bustling down the streets, going about their business.

It looked like normal London to Hamish. How did he

know Alex was telling the truth about all this?

And yet there was something a bit different about it.

'Hello!' said a man with a tiny suitcase under one arm, hurrying by, and patting Hamish's head as he did so.

'**Good afternoon!**' said a lady with a tuba, nodding her head and tipping her hat and beaming at them.

Hamish noticed that the word '**WELCOME**' on the sign had been underlined six times in felt tip – like the passers-by who'd done it really *meant* it.

This was a very friendly London indeed.

'All these people,' Hamish said, pointing at men patting other men on the back, and women smiling happily at one another. 'Do they know? Do they know they're Neverpeople? The people we *nearly* were?'

Alex hailed a cab. It was luminous yellow.

Hamish suddenly noticed that *all* the taxis were brightly coloured.

Very brightly coloured.

Why weren't they all black, like at home?

'When Henrietta Ford sold her first car,' said Alex, 'she said you can have any colour you like, so long as it *isn't* black!'

'Henri*etta* Ford!' said Hamish, delighted. Wait until Mr Slackjaw heard about this!

'Jump in, love,' said the taxi driver, adjusting her mirror. 'Where to?'

'A tour of the city, please, driver,' said Alex.

Hamish and Alice stared out of the window. What they saw amazed them.

Happy people poured out of department stores like *Jane* Lewis, or shops like *Master* Selfridge. Others stood patiently in queues in Burger *Queen*, or next to vans selling *Mrs* Whippy ice creams.

At Trafalgar Square, huge stone lionesses sat smiling at the foot of Horatia Nelson's column, celebrating her victory over Nancy Bonaparte at the Battle of Waterloo-seat-down-please.

Hamish spotted the London Eye in the distance – but was it revolving the opposite way now?

There was a statue of the famous nurse Fred Nightingale!

And over there – signs pointed towards Big Ben (except it was called Big Bertha now, named after a famous lady boxer from the 1800s) which was just round the corner from St Pauline's Cathedral.

There was *Victor* Station. There was a big statue of King Victor himself, looking very stern and shampooing his enormous beard.

Now they were passing Buckingham Palace.

'Look!' said Alice.

Behind the huge ornate gates, dozens of tall women in bearskin hats and bright red coats stood guard.

'Our most ferocious warriors,' explained Alex. 'Here to protect the King!'

'The *King*?' said Hamish and Alice in unison. They'd always grown up with a Queen!

'Yes,' said Alex. 'King Les the Second. He is . . . an *unusual* character. A wonderfully . . . *talkative* man. He has his own . . . *unique* sense of fashion.'

Hamish and Alice got the sense she was trying to be polite.

'This is all so cool,' said Hamish, but Alice didn't look quite as happy when they stopped at traffic lights. 'What's wrong, Alice?'

She had her arms folded and was staring up at a big poster of a portly man in his Y-fronts holding up some sun-tan lotion and smiling.

'That's Ken Moss,' said Alex. 'Supermodel.'

'It all makes me uncomfortable,' said Alice, shaking her head. 'I mean, look over there.'

She pointed at another poster of Ken Moss, this time advertising washing-up liquid, still in his Y-fronts.

'Why is it, in our world, it's mainly women who seem to advertise washing-up liquid and stuff?' she said. 'How is that fair? My *dad* washes up at home. It sort of makes me angry. I think I prefer this world.'

That gave Hamish a thought.

'Is it just London that's like this, Alex?' he said. 'Or is it the whole planet?'

'The whole planet,' she said. 'From the Statue of Libert-he to the very top of the Her-malayan mountains. From WoManchester to AmsterMadam and back again.'

Hamish considered this, as a line long of milk floats overtook them. Milk seemed far more popular in this world.

'It's nice to know there's balance in the universe,' he said, and, at this, Alex sat up straight.

'But don't you see – that's exactly what the bad guys are trying to end!'

'What do you mean?' said Hamish.

'Stop the cab!' shouted Alex, as they passed the enormous, grand British Library. 'We can walk from here . . .'

As they walked through the gates, Alex explained the problem.

You see, you might think you're a whole person – yes, you! – but you are only *half* a person. Your opposite on Otherearth is your other half!

So if you're a girl then somewhere there's a boy version of you.

And if you're a boy then somewhere there's a girl.

So what would happen to you if something happened to your *otherhalf*?

You would be . . . unbalanced!

Fifty per cent of the person you were!

You would be . . . a *half*wit!

You would go . . .

'Blank!' said Hamish. 'That must be what happened to the Prime Minister! *That's* why he started going on about his pants!'

'Exactly!' said Alex. 'They zapped the Neverpeople's PM, which meant that *your* PM went all weird. They got everyone in Downing Street because *if they can stop the people in power, they can take over both our worlds!*'

Hamish shuddered.

'Who else are they after?' asked Alice, in awe.

'They started with the people we look up to,' replied Alex. 'The people we admire and respect!'

'Yes – the politicians!' said Alice.

'What? No!' said Alex. 'The reality TV stars. The pop stars. The actors.'

'Vapidia Sheen!' said Hamish, thinking about her blank eyes on people's big-screen TVs.

'Precisely!' said Alex. 'Have you ever noticed how those people never seem to actually say anything? They open their mouths, but it's all just nonsense? There are no ideas.

No opinions. Just blather?'

'Yes!' said Hamish, remembering the two-hour episode of *Life's a Dream with Vapidia Sheen* where she couldn't get out of a revolving door.

'It's because someone got to their otherhalf!' said Alex.

This was dreadful.

But who was out to get the Neverpeople?

And how were they doing it?

And how were Hamish and Alice supposed to stop them on their own?

All these questions flew through Hamish's head as they reached a bench in front of the library.

On it sat a girl of Hamish's age.

Even with her hoodie on, Hamish could see she had wild, messy black hair.

A bag like his.

And . . . was that a big *white* 'H' on her top?

She looked very familiar, but Hamish was certain they'd never met.

And then the girl looked up at him, with a very fierce frown indeed.

He could have fainted.

'Hamish,' said Alex, placing one hand on his shoulder. 'Meet Holly Ellerby.'

HOLLY

NAME: HOLLY ELLIE ELLERBY

CODENAME: The Revenger.

HOMETOWN: Sparkley, Britain's Fourth Most Exciting Town!

SPECIAL SKILLS: Fearlessness. Recklessness. Fearsomeness.

ALWAYS CARRIES: Finger of Fudge, her RevengePad and the watch her mum gave her.

SIGNATURE MOVE: Never EVER EVER forgetting if someone's been rude to her!

FAVOURITE FOOD: The noodles at Wagapapa.

13

You + Me = Us

The first thing Hamish noticed about Holly Ellerby – aside from the fact that they were the same size, had the same eyes, the same hair colour, the same eyebrows, the same trainers and were, well, *the same*! – was that she wasn't very friendly.

Hamish couldn't understand that. He was delighted to meet her!

'You're my *otherhalf*!' he said, beaming and amazed.

'Hmm,' she said, scratching her nose. 'Yes, we'll see.'

'But you are!' he said. 'It's ace! You're the girl version of me!'

'I am *not* a version of you!' she said. 'I am *me*!'

Truth was Holly Ellerby had been annoyed when she'd found out she was only half of something. She'd sworn straight away not to give this imposter even the time of day. But Alex had insisted they meet. She said Hamish would prove useful and that it was important they stuck together if they were to save the world.

Well, thought Holly, *he doesn't seem very useful. He seems . . . mild-mannered. Like he thinks about things, instead of acting on them.*

This was not a time for thought. It was a time for action!

'And who's this?' said Holly, gesturing at Alice, and scowling under her hood.

'I'm Alice Shepherd, actually,' said Alice, a little offended. 'Founding member of the Starkley **PDF**.'

'Ha!' said Holly. 'Alex filled me in. You lot think you had it hard with a bunch of silly WorldStoppers! Small-town stuff. Well, you ain't seen nothing yet.'

'Oh, really?' said Alice, who was not taking to this girl at all.

'Yes, really,' said Holly, taking a step towards her. 'If I were you, Alice Shepherd, I'd turn around and run back to Starkley.'

'Is that right?' said Alice, now taking a step towards Holly and going a bit red. 'Only *I* thought we were here because you *needed our help?*'

'That's enough,' said Alex, snapping her phone shut and stepping in just as the two girls were almost nose to nose. 'I have to get back to base. I've just heard that Mortimer

Ribbons has been zapped.'

'The *newsreader*?!' said Holly.

'Apparently, he went on TV and started crying because no one would buy him a pony,' she said, shaking her head. 'He's sixty-three.'

'Then go,' said Holly. 'I'll tell these two what I've found so far.'

'Wait!' said Hamish. 'What about my dad? You know where he is, don't you? Is he in London?'

Alex hesitated. Was this the right thing to do, to leave them here? Her phone beeped again.

'I'll be in touch,' she said, starting to run.

Holly looked at the others suspiciously for a moment.

'Okay – here we go . . .'

She brought out a ring binder from her bag marked

HOLLY'S IMPORTANT FINDINGS.

PAGE 1

Here is what we know.

A person might be walking along, completely innocently, and then ZAP! They go blank.

Hamish turned the page.

But there wasn't anything there.

'Where's the rest of it?' he said.

'That's all there is,' said Holly.

'Ha!' said Alice. 'Those are your important findings? That's it? We already know that!'

'Right!' said Holly. '*You're* going in the book.'

She whipped out a small black book marked **'REVENGEPAD'**.

'What's a RevengePad?' asked Alice, laughing.

'Anyone who annoys me or is rude to me in any way goes straight in the RevengePad until I can work out a suitable revenge,' said Holly, scribbling Alice's name into the book that seemed to contain *thousands* of others. 'Once you're in the book, there's no way out. Not unless I have my revenge!'

'That doesn't seem very . . .' Hamish started, but Holly stared at him with her pen in her hand and he thought better of it.

He looked over her shoulder as she scribbled furiously, adding Alice's name and crime to the list.

SNIPE GLOOM, age 11
DREADFUL CRIME: Borrowed a quid off me for a can of Tango. Never saw him again.
POTENTIAL REVENGE: Put clingfilm over his toilet just before he needs to go.

LITTLE TOMMY BOTTOMS, age 9

DREADFUL CRIME: Giggled when I tripped on a pen.

Potential Revenge: Wrap up every single one of his toys in tinfoil.

SCARPER RADISH, age 10

Dreadful Crime: Did not say 'bless you' when I sneezed.

Potential Revenge: I will sneeze in her ear and not cover my mouth.

'What is *wrong* with you?!' said Hamish, involuntarily.

'And anyway,' said Holly, putting the RevengePad back in her bag, 'that wasn't *all* my findings. It was all I had time to write down because I've been so busy exacting my revenge on people.'

'Well, what else do you know about these zappings?' asked Alice.

'I know who's behind them,' said Holly, looking up into the air mysteriously. 'And his name . . . is *Scarmarsh*.'

EVIL ICONS #437
Say Hello to 'Scarmarsh'!

by Windermere Van Grunt

Just who is Axel Scarmarsh, the newest bad boy on the scene?

'I like to think I'm just like any other evil icon,' says the evil icon, looking particularly evil and icon-like. 'Except just a little bit more evil and icon-like.'

Scarmarsh shot to global evil fame just two short years ago when he created an underground lair on the Scandinavian island of FRYKT.

'It was a place for me to relax and try new things,' he explains. 'Somewhere I could be myself. Which is incredibly evil and icon-like.'

Of course, we all know what that led to – the development of his own super-breed of terrifying monsters, the Terribles!

'The Global Evil Community was very excited when I unveiled the Terribles at the press conference in Magaluf,' he says. 'Particularly when I told them we were able to tunnel all the way from FRYKT to the coastline of Britain, where we found a tiny island near the insignificant town of Starkley.'

Why did he use a tunnel?

'Terribles aren't particularly fond of water,' he explains. 'It gets in their crevices and dampens their tusks. I'm working on it.'

His plans for Starkley, however, didn't quite work out the way he'd hoped.

'I don't want to talk about that,' he says, waving the question away. 'I'd rather concentrate on my future plans.'

These include a few modifications to the Terribles that he's keeping under wraps for now.

'Let's just say that as I look out over the world from on high, plans are afoot,' he says. 'I enjoy playing with time and space, and, since the whole WorldStoppers project, I have discovered a new and far more . . . targeted way to get things done.'

Can he give us any clues?

'I'm afraid not. But remember, sometimes the "opposite" is true . . .' he says, mysteriously, and then laughs his trademark evil laugh.

'Put it this way – I plan to teach the world a ROYAL lesson! One the whole world will see at once! Only THEN will Scarmarsh be CROWNED the NEW AND RIGHTFUL LEADER OF THE WORLD!'

LATEST FROM FRYKT

'Watch Out' for Hypnobots! p.16

THE EYES HAVE IT
Belasko technology stolen! p.11

DRINK BLILK
It's not good for you, but it's cheap. p.76

'So it's him?' said Hamish, appalled. 'It's this Scarmarsh guy? He's the one zapping people and turning them blank? Where did you find this?'

Holly folded up the photocopied magazine article and put it back in her bag.

'The British Library. There's a hidden vault at the back. Alex gave me the code. I've been casing the joint for days.'

Hamish was amazed at how confident Holly seemed with all this. He wouldn't know the first thing about casing a joint. He'd feel very awkward doing that, he decided, in case someone came up and asked him what he was doing and he had to reply, 'Oh, just casing a joint.' And the only library he knew much about was the one in school. He certainly didn't know that the British Library keeps a copy of almost every single book, newspaper and magazine published in the country. And not just this country. There are 150 million items in there – some of them more than 3000 years old!

And right at the back, down a staircase, and then another staircase, is a statuette of the Earth. Look very closely and you'll see a Belasko logo just above Portugal. Lift that statuette up and there's a panel. Type in the right code and . . .

'The wall slides away,' said Holly. 'And inside is every copy

of every underground, secret-society newspaper, newsletter and magazine that has ever been published . . . *including* Evil Icon *magazine.*'

'So Scarmarsh was responsible for the WorldStoppers,' said Alice. 'He's some kind of evil inventor?'

'Some say he's a scientist. Others that he's a Duke. When the WorldStoppers failed in their mission, Scarmarsh fled to Otherearth to hide among the Neverpeople and continue his work.'

'What kind of work?' asked Hamish, hoping she might say 'gardening' or 'setting up a small dating website'.

'*Evil* work,' she replied. 'He once developed a shrink ray that could shrink *anything!* He shrank down two Ferraris so that he could stand on them and then used them as high-powered roller skates!'

'That's pretty cool!' said Hamish, and both Holly and Alice punched him on the arm because apparently that *wasn't* cool, that was dastardly.

But, even though they'd done precisely the same thing for precisely the same reason, Alice and Holly now fumed at each other.

'*Don't* punch Hamish,' said Alice, put out. 'He's my best friend!'

'Don't *you* punch Hamish!' replied Holly, angrily. 'He's half me!'

They really weren't getting on.

'But what does Scarmarsh mean,' said Hamish, trying to change the subject and avoid a fight, 'when he says he wants to teach the world a royal lesson? One the whole world will see?'

'Think about it,' said Holly, putting her hands on her hips. 'So far he's been zapping Prime Ministers, politicians, pop stars and anyone who's famous or has power . . . and who is even *more* famous than the Prime Minister?'

Hamish racked his brains. Beyoncé?

Wait!

'Royalty!' he said. 'He wants to zap royalty! That's his royal lesson!'

'I think he wants to zap our King,' said Holly. 'And that means he can get your Queen at the same time.'

'But why hasn't he done it already?' asked Alice. 'Surely, if he could zap the Prime Minister, he could have zapped the King?'

'I don't know,' said Holly. 'All I know is King Les is due to appear in public tomorrow night at 6 p.m. to make an important speech, and if Scarmarsh says he wants the *whole world* to see then my guess would be *that's* when he'll strike . . .'

14

The Isle of Dogs

Well, well, well. How about that! Told you that you were going to be reading about things that could make your feet fall off! Bet you wished you'd stopped reading earlier, don't you?

No?

Well, if you're so brave, then let's crack on!

'I still don't know what this has to do with my dad,' said Hamish, as the three of them jumped on a red London bus away from the station, and a plan started to form in Hamish's mind.

'Same thing it has to do with my mum, I guess,' said Holly, sadly.

'Oh, of course,' said Hamish, realising that if Holly was the other half of him then her life would be similar too. 'So your mum . . .'

'Disappeared,' said Holly, leaning her head against the window. 'On Boxing Day.'

Alice didn't know what to say. Maybe this was why Holly always seemed so angry.

'Wait,' said Hamish. 'Do you think our mum and dad are together somewhere? Maybe they're in hiding? Maybe Scarmarsh is trying to get them!'

It made perfect sense. Alex had said Hamish's dad had knowledge the bad guys wanted, and that he was the only one that could stop them. Hamish stood up, feeling slightly braver, and knowing it was down to him, Alice and Holly to save the King.

'We need reinforcements,' he said, very forcefully. 'We need to go back to Starkley and get the **PDF**!'

'What? No!' said Holly. 'We're supposed to stick together! Alex said!'

'Then come with us!'

Holly thought about it.

'Our friend Elliot is a genius,' said Alice. 'He'll work out how Scarmarsh is doing this. Clover is a master of disguise. She'll help us move around without getting zapped. Buster is brilliant with technology – if that's what Scarmarsh is using, he'll know just what to do. And Venk . . .'

'Yes?' said Holly.

'. . . well, I'm sure we can find something for Venk to do.'

'Sounds precisely the *opposite* of all my pals,' said Holly.

'And Alice,' said Hamish. 'We could really do with your uncle's help.'

'My uncle?' said Alice, surprised. 'Oh, yes, my, um, uncle.'

'You said your Uncle Peter is a policeman in Shaddington.'

'Shaddington?' said Holly, scrunching up her nose.

'Well, we need to tell him,' continued Hamish. 'He's a policeman so he can help us warn the King! Who else would believe us?'

'Er, thing is . . .' said Alice. 'My Uncle Peter . . .'

'Yes?' said Hamish.

Alice looked at her friend. And then at Holly, who was smiling at her, but not in a good way. Alice took a deep breath.

'I made him up.'

'You . . . you *made him up*?'

'Sorry, Hamish. I just knew there was no way your mum would have let you come to London if—'

Hamish's eyes widened.

'*Mum!* Wait – what time is it?'

He looked at his watch. It was nearly six o'clock!

'We should have been on the way home by now!' he said, panicking. 'And instead we're on a big red bus in a totally different dimension! Mum'll definitely call the police! Or phone your parents and ask for your Uncle Peter's phone number and find out you fibbed!'

He turned to Holly and looked her deep in the eyes.

'Holly – we've got to go back now, before my mum goes mad. Are you coming with us to Starkley or are we leaving you behind?'

'*Fine*,' said Holly, annoyed. 'But there's one of us missing.'

Hamish counted. No, there were three of them. Hamish wasn't great at maths, but he was pretty sure on this one.

'Who?' said Hamish, confused. '*Who's missing?*'

Holly smiled, and looked at Alice.

ЖЖ

They were heading for the Isle of Dogs.

From a distance, this part of London looked very modern. It was surrounded by river, and the top of the huge skyscraper, Canary Wharf, blinked in the darkening sky. But the kids were going further, down to the old factories by the docks.

Holly didn't seem at all concerned, but both Hamish and Alice found it all a little eerie. Hamish couldn't shake the feeling he was being watched.

There seemed to be no one else around, yet strange shapes shifted on the other side of the river. Workmen in orange hard hats with little lights on were digging a hole, while a postman trundled by with a trolley, whistling badly. They all tipped their hats at each other, and somewhere a dog barked.

'Alan Shepherd didn't feel safe walking around town,' explained Holly, as she guided them down a barely-lit path.

'Oh, yes,' said Alice, sarcastically. 'This seems *far* safer.'

'He may be your otherhalf,' said Holly, 'but he's a little nervous about getting zapped. He said he felt more comfortable being indoors, around people he can trust. I suppose if they *did* zap him, you'd end up even sillier than you are already.'

At this, Alice took great offence. She turned to face Holly full on.

'Let me tell you something, Hollyollerby. I mean Holl-*ololby*. I mean Holler-ellarbelly. I mean *Holly*. If Alan Shepherd is *anything* like me, he is a *survivor*. He has many talents. He can think on his feet. He will be *fine*.'

Holly made an awkward face.

'He's really not like you at all,' she said, and she pointed at a large sign on a factory door behind them.

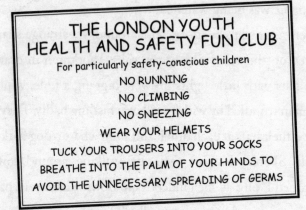

THE LONDON YOUTH
HEALTH AND SAFETY FUN CLUB
For particularly safety-conscious children
NO RUNNING
NO CLIMBING
NO SNEEZING
WEAR YOUR HELMETS
TUCK YOUR TROUSERS INTO YOUR SOCKS
BREATHE INTO THE PALM OF YOUR HANDS TO
AVOID THE UNNECESSARY SPREADING OF GERMS

'This place sounds rubbish!' said Alice.

'Alan's already been made Executive Vice Chairman,' said Holly. 'He only joined this morning. But they won't give him a badge because badges have pins.'

'What do you do in a Health and Safety fun club?' asked Hamish, a little befuddled.

'You mainly talk about Health and Safety,' said Holly. 'But at a volume considered acceptable according to international safety guidelines.'

'It's in a bit of a dangerous area for a Health and Safety club!' said Alice, looking around, just as confused. Bins were knocked over; shopping trollies had been left all over the place; there was glass on the pavements and dog poo *everywhere*.

'Alan told me there are only three members, and they don't believe in charging for it because you can be allergic to the metal they put in five-pound notes. This place is all they can afford.'

'Well, I'm sure Alan is just fine,' replied Alice, defensively. 'I'm sure he's a terrific kid who shines in his own way. I'm sure he stands out, makes his presence known. I'm sure he—'

'Hello,' said a small voice, quite timidly.

No one had noticed that a smaller boy had been right next to them the whole time. He was rather pale and sickly, with droopy hair and arms that seemed too heavy to lift.

He was wearing a helmet. Shin guards. Arm protectors.

He had an American football top on with great big shoulder pads.

His trousers were tucked into his socks to prevent unnecessary trippage.

And he had one bright ~~turquoyse~~ aquamarine line through his hair. (His mum put it there so that drivers could see him in the dark. No sense risking it.)

'Have you been out here the whole time?' said Holly.

ALAN

NAME: ALAN 'MY MIDDLE NAME IS SAFETY' SHEPHERD
CODENAME: Alan *Shhhhhh*-keep-your-voice-down-epherd.
SPECIAL SKILLS:
The Quiver, the Leggit, the See-you-late
SECRET FACT:
Alan believes it is safer not to have secret
But he keeps that to himself.

'Why didn't you go in?'

'I didn't want to try the door in case I trapped my finger,' said Alan.

'No,' said Alice, shaking her head. 'No, you're not—'

'I'm Alan,' said the boy. 'I won't shake your hand because that is actually the number-one way in which germs are passed from one person to another and I don't actually know if you're the sort of person who washes their hands after they've been to the toilet.'

'Of *course* I'm the sort of person who washes their hands after they've been to the toilet!' said Alice, but then she had to squint as she tried to remember if that was definitely true.

'I can't believe my otherhalf is such a dweeb!' she said.

'*I* can,' said Holly, and Alice scowled at her.

'I really think we should be in a more brightly-lit area,' said Alan.

'We will be, Alan,' said Hamish. 'Come on, let's go.'

The four of them started to walk to the main road.

'So we'll get the bus back to Arcadian Lane,' said Hamish. 'Once we're in our world, I'll call Mum and say we've been delayed, and then we'll get the coach to Starkley.'

'Back to your world?' said Alan, worried. 'I'm not sure I should go all the way back to your world. I shouldn't even have come to the city. But Holly said it was important. She said we had to come to find out what had happened to her mum and that she needed moral support.'

Hamish looked at Holly. She must want just the same answers he did. They were definitely different, but they also had their similarities. He tried to give her a reassuring smile, but she didn't want it. She constantly wore a look of grim determination that Hamish wished he had too.

'Anyway,' said Alan, 'we tracked down Alex and she said if we were here then it might not be long before *you* turned up, and if you did we had to stick together to protect each other and I've always said there's safety in numbers, and—'

But Hamish wasn't listening any more. Because at the end

of the road he had spotted something unusual.

'What's that?' he said.

The whole street was lit by a spinning blue light.

They could hear the crackle of a radio.

'The police!' said Holly, pointing at a huge white van surrounded by a dozen or so police officers with their backs to them.

'Look!' whispered Alice, shocked.

On a lamp post was a poster.

There were pictures of all four of them!

'Mum must have called the police,' said Hamish, his tummy turning and swirling. He was in trouble. And he hated the idea of his mum worrying. He'd really let her down. This whole thing had been stupid. But he'd just got carried away, and it was important, and it was for Dad, and maybe she'd understand.

'I'd better go and talk to them,' he said, his stomach sinking.

'Good idea!' said Alan.

'NO!' said Alice and Holly at once.

'Think about it, H,' said Alice. 'Your mum's in a different world! It doesn't make sense for the police to be looking for us here.'

'Unbelievably, Alice is right!' said Holly. 'How do the Otherearth police even know you're here?'

And, as the blue light kept swirling round, Hamish looked a little harder . . .

And a little harder . . .

It was dark now, but he could see one policeman, in particular, who was blowing on a polystyrene cup of tea, trying to cool it down. The steam was rising into the air.

'You know,' said Hamish, uncertainly, 'that policeman sort of looks like . . .'

And now that policeman caught sight of *him*.

He turned, slowly, staring straight back at Hamish, who suddenly was filled with nothing but fear, and dread, and **TERROR** as he saw the policeman's face properly for the first time and realised . . .

That wasn't steam rising from the tea.

That was steam coming *from the policeman*!

Oh, no! *Oh dear, no!*

'Why does that policeman have tusks?' asked Alan.

'*Run!*' said Holly, as the 'policeman' threw down his cup of tea and **ROARED** to alert his friends. '*RUN!*'

Ruuuuun!

'**RUUUUUUUUUUN!**' screamed Alice, as the gang rounded a corner. '*Ruuuuun!*'

There was really no need to keep shouting it. Everyone was running.

'**RUUUUUUUUN!**' she shouted again.

'But remember to look where you're going!' said Alan, keenly, making sure to keep his knees up and his back straight, as back pain is the number-one cause of work-related absence in Britain. 'And are we really sure that running is the best course of action? Only statistics prove that—'

'**SHUT UP AND RUN, ALAN!**' shouted everybody else, all at once.

The **SCREEALS** and **SCREECHES** of their pursuers grew with every second.

Hamish was struggling to make sense of it all.

That policeman had looked just like . . . a Terrible!

123

Those ghastly, gluttonous, gelatinous beasts that tried to take over Starkley!

But these ones looked different somehow. They looked *angrier*.

'Round this corner!' yelled Alice. 'Look!'

A rickety old sign pointed towards Dog Walk.

'Dog Walk was on the Unorthodox Line! I remember Leo mentioning it! We can catch a train back to Arcadian Lane and get home through The Gap!'

The foot tunnel was straight ahead. It ran directly under the river, which meant they could use it to escape the Isle of Dogs. The tunnel was very long and barely lit.

'I don't understand what's happening!' said Alan, struggling to keep his helmet on. 'And we should really stop running now because we didn't warm up properly!'

'The Terribles!' shouted Hamish, looking behind him in case the beasts were upon them. 'They're back – and this time they're in disguise!'

Let me ask you this: when was the last time you saw a policeman?

Tuesday?

Really?

Gosh, you've got a good memory.

And do you remember what the policeman looked like?

Well, of course you do. He was wearing a policeman's uniform, wasn't he?

Yes. I can picture him now. Standing there, with a policeman's hat on, looking all policeman-like.

But think back . . .

Do you remember what he *actually* looked like?

Like, what kind of face did he have? Or was it a she?

Was it a friendly face? A grumpy one?

I bet you don't remember. Not really. Because all you actually looked at was the uniform, wasn't it? After all, that's all you *needed* to look at to know it was a policeman or woman.

But here's the awful truth: most of the time we're too comfortable. We look but we don't see.

And that's exactly what the Terribles are banking on.

They know we're too lazy to look at everyone we pass. And they know we won't bother looking too closely at them if we think we've already seen them.

That's why they wear the uniforms: so that when we *see* them, we don't really *look* at them.

That guy? Oh, he's just a policeman.

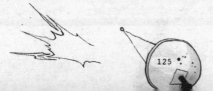

Her? She's a soldier. Or a surgeon.

Him? He's a postman.

Her? She's a Cub Scout leader. Or a pilot. Or a builder.

That chap over by the bins? Don't worry about him. He's a nurse. Or he works in McDonald's. Or he's a baker. Or maybe he's just a weird old clown standing at your window.

Actually, that last one's absolutely terrifying – please forget I said that.

You see, the Terribles know that if there's a coat to be worn, they should wear it. And if there's a hat to be donned, they should don it.

If they dress like us, we'll think they *are* us. What else could they be?

Just some workmen in orange hard hats with little lights on, after dark. Just a postman, whistling badly as he pushes a trolley around – even though it's night!

So yes: the Terribles were back. They walk among us.

And I'll ask you again. When was the last time you saw a policeman?

Because what if the last time you saw a policeman you'd looked a little closer . . .

and you'd seen those globulous, spiked, greasy hands . . .

those wet black eyes . . .

those teeth . . .

those scales . . .

What if what you *really* saw . . . was a Terrible?

'They're coming!' yelled Hamish, as the gang made it out
of the foot tunnel. Dog Walk was down the hill, some
distance away, but at least now they could *see* it. The streets
were dirty here too. There was rubbish on the ground and
an abandoned shopping trolley from Fathercare had been
pushed up against a tree.

Hamish checked behind them. The Terribles had made it
into the tunnel. They had paused for a second before they
did, he was sure of it. But there wasn't time to think about
why they stopped because now they were bounding at speed
behind them. He could make out vast trails of saliva and
spit being flung from their horrible mouths, coating the
walls of the tunnel.

He realised they weren't going to make it. The Terribles
were faster than they'd ever been. How could they get away?

'Quick! The shopping trolley!' shouted Holly, pulling it
from the tree and climbing inside.

'Absolutely not!' said Alan, backing away. 'Do you know
how dangerous those are? There aren't even any brakes!'

'What do you think is more dangerous?' said Alice, hopping in. 'A shopping trolley or a vast army of slobulous monsters?'

Alan did the maths in his head and came to the same conclusion as Alice. She pulled him on board by the seat of his pants.

'Push, Hamish!' shouted Holly. 'Push!'

And Hamish pushed. He pushed hard, then jumped on the back.

The shopping trolley began to pick up speed as it trundled down the hill . . . and soon the trundle was a *zoom* . . .

'We're getting faster!' shouted Hamish, now clinging on for dear life. 'But how do we stop it?'

Just then, one of the wheels clipped a stone, and the shopping trolley began to spin round and round and round . . .

'I didn't think about stopping!' shouted Holly, panicking, and feeling rather sick. 'There's no steering wheel either!'

Hamish's mum had been worried that this exact thing might happen! Mums worry about some pretty specific stuff, don't they?

As the trolley spun wildly round, they saw Dog Walk Station . . . then the Terribles . . . then Dog Walk . . . then the Terribles . . . then Dog Walk!

'We're going to crash!' shouted Alan. 'I knew this would happ—'

CRASH!

They smashed through the old wooden doors of the Ghost Station. Inside, the tiled floor was flat and smooth and the trolley showed no signs of slowing. They shot across the lobby of Dog Walk and into the tunnels marked **TO THE TRAINS**. It was like they were on a rollercoaster! The trolley slammed against the handrail, which sparked as it guided them round and down the walkway, down further and further, deeper and deeper . . .

The wind rose . . . a hot blast of air hitting their faces, meaning a train had just arrived!

SMAK-ASH! The Terribles crashed through the broken doors of Dog Walk, slippering and skattering their nails on the tiles.

'We need to get on that train!' shouted Alice, as the trolley continued to grind and spark against the handrail and whizzed further and further down into the depths of the station. 'How close are the Terribles?'

But she needn't have asked: the shadows behind them were looming larger as they reached the end of the foot tunnel and . . .

BANG!
The trolley hit the bottom of the train and flung the four kids straight through the open doors of the carriage.

They sat there, dazed, for a second.

'*This* is why people should wear helmets!' yelled Alan, delighted to be at last proved right. 'I told you, Holly!'

Holly frowned. 'Right, I'm *sorry*, Alan,' she said, whipping out her RevengePad, 'but you're going in the book.'

'Shhhh!' said Hamish. '*Listen!*'

The Terribles were very close now. They were clattering down the walkway in hot pursuit. Just because the kids were on a train didn't mean they were safe.

Hamish could not just hear the beasts, but smell them now too. That familiar, acrid smell that stung his eyes and went straight to his stomach.

'How do we close the doors?' cried Alice.

'They're automatic!' said Hamish, willing them to shut, as the tunnel in front of them filled with shadows. 'They're—'

BEEP BEEP BEEEEEP sang the doors, as the first of the Terribles made it round the corner and flipped the shopping trolley out of the way. It flew through the air and skittered down the platform . . . just as the doors closed.

For a second, there was silence.

The four kids cowered inside the train carriage.

They backed away, as more and more Terribles filled the

131

station. One of them – wearing a sergeant's outfit – slapped a greasy, wet hand on to the train window. Some pressed their faces up against the glass and tried to use bony fingers to slice round the edges with a low **GRRRRRRROOOWL**. The clatter of their toenails on the tiles filled the air. Steam rose from their bodies.

'Holly,' stuttered Hamish. 'Give me your RevengePad and pen!'

'I don't think they'll feel very threatened by that,' she said, but handed it over.

Hamish quickly drew something on the Pad, and then held it up to the window.

It was a sunflower. Hamish knew from his previous encounter with these things that if there was one thing they feared, it was sunflowers. That was why Starkley was covered in them these days – to make sure the Terribles never came back.

The giant Terrible in the sergeant's uniform stared at it through the glass, fogging it up with his breath.

It jolted its head back immediately when it spotted the sunflower.

But not because it was scared.

Because it was *laughing*!

132

BUH-HUUUUU-HUUUUUU
UUURRRRRR!

It was then that Hamish realised something awful. These weren't like the Terribles he'd seen before. Those Terribles had lived on good country air and clean country water, from the fields and forests around Starkley.

But these . . . these were *City* Terribles.

They were Terribles who'd spent months in the dark and soot beneath London, biding their time.

Their backs were blackened by the diesel juice that coated the underground tunnels they'd stalk and stride through. Their tempers were blackened too, from constantly electrifying themselves on the rails of the old lines.

Their lungs had filled with the concrete dust from building works that made them wheeze and rasp as they ran, so that they sounded like they were permanently GRRRRROWLING.

Those eyes that you could see were bloodshot and yellowed.

Those fingers were cracked and splintery.

If a Country Terrible was like a huge, stupid dog, a City Terrible was like a *panther*.

Low. Muscular. Intimidating. Quick to anger. Thinking Terrible thoughts and doing Terrible things. These were the most terrible Terribles yet.

And then – finally! – the train began to rev and REV and REV and, as the Terribles started to crack the glass of the weakening windows, it **SHOT OFF** towards Arcadian Lane with a **POW!**

16

OMG

These were some pretty shocked kids.

I mean *shocked* shocked.

Super *crazy* shocked.

Shocked squared!

Well, wouldn't *you* be shocked? Chased around and grabbed at by awful, monstrous beasts?

If you'd seen the four of them as they got off the train at Arcadian Lane, or as they found their way back to Victoria Station here on Earth, or as they clambered on to the coach marked STARKLEY, you would have noticed them for sure.

Their eyes were massive, for a start. It was like they couldn't blink any more. They were just staring.

Alan tried to open a can of Coke, but he was shaking so much it just exploded and all the drink flew out.

That had happened three times so far. He was soaked.

Now, as the coach found the motorway, Holly broke the silence.

'Well, thanks for the tip, Hamish,' she said. 'Next time I'm in mortal danger, remind me to take a moment to quickly draw a flower.'

Hamish blushed. He had really thought the sunflower would work.

'It's strange how our worlds are so similar but so different,' continued Holly, looking out of the window at the shops and people and places.

Alan tried to open another drink and it just exploded all over him again. Gently, Alice reached over and opened the next one for him. They shared a small smile.

There was a newspaper on the floor.

'*The Sun*,' said Holly. 'I suppose that must be your version of one of *our* papers.'

'Oh, yeah?' said Hamish. 'Which one?'

'*The Daughter*,' said Holly. 'Hey – look . . .'

The headline read: **NOW THE CHIEF OF POLICE GOES WEIRD** over a picture of Chief Superintendent Valerie Snump trying to kiss and cuddle a small rubber chicken.

To one side was a picture of Buckingham Palace.

'What's your Queen like?' asked Holly, pointing to the picture.

'Oh, she's very polite. Quite quiet. Keeps herself to herself.

Usually just makes a speech once a year at Christmas. Just to let us know what she's been up to and ask how we're doing.'

'Just one speech! Wow. You're lucky.'

'Why?' asked Alice. 'How many does your King make?'

Holly and Alan rolled their eyes.

'He's always on about something,' said Alan, and it was true. King Les the Second was an extraordinarily chatty King, who didn't seem to mind what you chatted about, so long as it was him that could do most of the chatting.

You could point at anything and he could chat about it.

Trees.

Beef.

Your dad's hairy nose.

He had a fact about everything too.

'Did you know that you can't lick your own elbow?' he'd shout, from his royal motorbike-and-sidecar, as he was driven through Billingsgate Fish Market. 'I command you to try it!'

And all the fishmongers would drop their fish and try to lick their elbows, all at once.

You try it.

HA! You see? King Les is right! You can't lick your own elbow!

Did you know that when a penguin proposes, he gives his mate a pebble?

It's TRUE! King Les told that to the Queen of Denmark and her ears went red – that's how amazed she was!

Did you know that humans get taller in space because there's no gravity pushing them down?

Did you know your eyeball weighs about the same as thirty paper clips?!

Did you know? No!

King Les loved the phrase 'Did You Know?' so much that

he had it translated into Latin and put on his coat of arms.

NONNE SCITIS it says.

Which actually sounds more like something you'd catch.

But King Les's greatest dream was to be asked on *Well, Whaddya Know? The TV quiz show with all the answers!* (To be fair, it would be a pretty rubbish TV show if it was the quiz show *without* all the answers. It'd just be half an hour of questions and then everyone would go home again.)

The problem was, King Les knew they wouldn't let him on. First, because he was the King and it wouldn't be fair. And second because if he didn't know the answer to one of the questions he still had the power to lock all the people who made the show in the Tower.

So King Les spent most of his time just learning interesting facts and then choosing his outfits. Today he was wearing a one-piece lime-green catsuit with a bright red cape, blue sunglasses and large white basketball boots. He looked like he'd got dressed in the dark. In a charity shop. In a hurry.

The sad thing was King Les just wanted to be normal sometimes. He didn't feel at all comfortable being King. So how did he end up in that position? It's not like he went down the job centre or answered an advert in the post-office window. It's not like he started off as a Junior King or an

Assistant King and then worked his way up to be Boss King.

No!

He was just taken aside one day by his mum, who said, 'Look, I'm fed up being Queen. I want to watch telly all day.' And then she tagged him and said, 'You're it!' and ran away. She's still hiding in an upstairs bedroom to this day, just in case he tags her back.

That's the way Kings and Queens had been decided for generations. So many Royals got a bit fed up with the attention or felt a little embarrassed about all the unearned money that they tagged someone else and ran off to hide. There was a rumour that King Victor himself was still holed up in the attic somewhere, hiding in a grandmother clock.

So now Les had this whole blooming country to oversee. Have you ever had to oversee a whole country? Probably not. But it's hard work and, to add to the problem, no one much liked any of Les's ideas.

He wanted to change the flag to something a bit more imaginative, like a huge purple triangle with a bright gold sausage in the middle.

But everyone said no.

He wanted to have giant oil paintings all over the palace, of cool stuff like a horse riding a bicycle over a rainbow with a badger on its back.

But everyone said no.

King Les was always having his ideas knocked back. Mind you, King Les was always full of dreadful ideas. That's why *some* of the staff secretly called him 'King *Les*-said-about-that-guy-the-better!'.

'He sounds like a nightmare!' said Alice, being very honest. 'No wonder Scarmarsh wants to zap him.'

Holly thought about it.

'Funny he's not done it before now, though,' she said, warming to Alice a little more. 'Maybe he wants more people to witness it? Like he did with your Prime Minister on live TV?'

Of course, it hadn't just been Ernst Ding-Batt who'd been zapped that night. It was his otherhalf too, remember. Poor *Ernabell* Ding-Batt had been blanked at the same time, and now thought her best friend was a tea cosy named Captain Dullard.

'Holly, you said you thought Scarmarsh was planning something tomorrow. What exactly is the King *doing*?' asked Hamish, searching for clues.

'He's getting his new crown,' said Holly, leaning her head against the window. 'He's so excited that he's been telling anyone who'll listen. He sent off for it ages ago, but it's taken forever to arrive. Les has been wearing a temporary one lately, but he really wants his big gold and silver one.'

'Oh,' said Hamish, and then he had a thought. 'Will it be on TV?'

'Yes,' said Holly. 'It's on straight after *Life's a Bad Dream with Vermin Sheen*.'

'And where's it happening?' asked Alice, now sitting up, as she realised that all this might be very important information indeed.

'The Tower,' said Holly, as the sign for **STARKLEY** came into view. 'It's all happening at the Tower of London.'

'Then that's when Scarmarsh will strike,' said Hamish, looking grave. 'And only the **PDF** can stop him!'

17

PDF Ahoy!

Hamish trudged back to 13 Lovelock Close with a heavy heart.

He knew he was in trouble.

Huge trouble.

Humungous trouble.

Trouble might as well be his middle name.

He'd phoned his mum as soon as he'd got back to our world, of course. But she hadn't been in at the time because she does heavy metal yoga on Tuesdays at the leisure centre in Frinkley. So he'd left a message and felt sick all the way back to town.

'Oh my gosh,' said Holly, stunned, as she looked around Starkley, which appeared to be shut. 'This place is so boring!'

Hamish was a little offended.

'It's not, actually,' he said.

But next to him was a poster for this week's *Starkley Post* and the headline was **<u>MOVE ON, NOTHING</u>**

<u>TO SEE HERE</u>, which sort of contradicted him.

Alan had gone back to Alice's house with her. 'Safety in numbers!' he said every five seconds, and Alice wanted to keep him where she could see him. Alan kept asking if the spare bed had rails round the side because he prefers a bed with rails round the side: what if he fell out?

'Don't fall out then,' said Alice, churlishly. 'Or just keep your helmet on.'

'Oh, I fully intend to wear a sleep helmet,' said Alan, nodding. Alice just rolled her eyes.

Holly had agreed to wait outside Hamish's house at first, just until he could explain everything to his mum.

He had absolutely no idea how he was going to do that. Or how much to tell her because, if she was worried about Hamish before, when he told her about travelling to a different dimension, she was going to be *livid*.

'Good luck,' said Holly, and after one deep breath Hamish pushed open the door. 'I'll just stay out here, in this thrilling town.'

Hamish could hear the TV as he stepped inside.

But wait, what else was that he could hear?

Laughter?

He walked into the living room to find his mum in fits of

giggles, slapping the table and hooting.

He'd never heard his mum hoot before.

'*Haaaaamish!*' she said, flinging her arms round him and beaming. 'Welcome home, chicken!'

Over her shoulder, he saw that sitting in the chair right behind her with a cup of coffee and a chocolate Mustn'tgrumble . . . was Alex.

She winked at him.

'Alex explained everything!' said his mum, giving him a thumbs up. 'What an adventure! What fun! Did you know Alex works for Belasko, Dad's old company?'

Hamish scrunched up his nose. This did not seem like a normal reaction. Why wasn't he in trouble? Even *he* thought he should be in trouble.

On the TV, a blank-eyed newsreader stared straight ahead, not saying anything. *They got another one*, thought Hamish.

'Tell me about London!' said Mum. 'Did you go to the zoo? How was the Prime Minister? Did you eat a kebab? I hear you have to go back! Do you want me to make you a sandwich?'

Hamish shot Alex a look.

What was going on?

Hamish's mum was fast asleep on the sofa three minutes later.

'It's a new type of coffee,' said Alex, pointing at the packet on the table. 'We call it **BELASKOFFEE**. It's very . . . relaxing. Packed with chamomile. We originally developed it for agents who we knew were going to face monsters. It lets them see the funny side. Cope with anything. I thought maybe your mum could do with a cup. I know how she worries. That's why your dad could never tell her what his secret *real* job was.'

'Well, it seems to work,' said Hamish, looking at his mum, who was now snoring and drooling. 'Mum seems to have found it very relaxing indeed.'

'I told her you'd need to make another trip,' said Alex.

'How did you know where I was?' he asked, and Alex smiled.

'I have my ways of watching you,' she said. 'Now go – it's time you told the rest of your friends that we need their help.'

ЖЖ

'*Elliot!*' whispered Hamish, as loudly as you can before it becomes not a whisper any more. '*Wake up!*'

He'd already fetched Alice.

They'd been to wake Buster.

And Clover. And Venk.

They'd accidentally woken Grenville too, because he lived next door to Venk and had *insisted* on coming.

'I'm an honorary member of the **PDF**!' he kept saying. 'And I'm the one who knows the most wrestling moves!'

Now they were all standing outside Elliot's house at almost midnight, throwing small pebbles at his window.

'What in the name of *Thor*?' said Elliot, opening his window. He looked down and saw:

Hamish, with a look of grim determination on his face.

Clover, already holding her emergency fake moustaches.

Venk, combing his hair, ready for action.

Buster, holding a golden spanner.

Grenville, inspecting a remarkable bogey.

And Alice, tapping her watch and beckoning him down, impatiently.

'I have to say, I've been hoping for quite some time that we'd get the **PDF** back together,' said Elliot, leading everyone down the path in his back garden. 'I thought it had all ended.'

'Every end is just another beginning!' said Alice.

'I thought that too, so I did a little preparation.'

Elliot was very good at preparation. Every member of the **PDF** brought something different to the team. Buster was a technical genius, Clover was a master of disguise, Venk . . . I'll get back to you on that . . . and Elliot was in charge of strategies and operations. And, even though the Pauses had stopped, Elliot had kept himself busy – just in case of an emergency.

He switched on the light in the long shed at the bottom of his garden and Hamish's jaw dropped.

In front of him on a table was a gigantic map of the country.

There were little statuettes of the gang that could be moved around on top of it using a long pointer.

There were beautiful paintings of all the awful types of Terribles they'd encountered.

There was a computer and a printer and all manner of strange devices.

A huge sign on the wall read **WAR ROOM**.

'I've had quite a lot of time on my hands,' said Elliot, shyly.

'Ah*em*,' came a small voice from behind them.

Hamish had asked Holly to keep her distance for the time being.

Everybody now turned to see her standing in the doorway,

with a timid Alan cowering behind her.

'Who's that?' asked Clover.

'Hey . . . that girl looks a lot like *you*, Hamish . . .' said Elliot, pushing his glasses up his nose.

Everyone looked at Hamish, and blinked.

He realised he had rather a lot of explaining to do.

'This is the most incredible thing I have ever heard!' said Grenville, minutes later. 'And *I* once heard a dog say "sausages"!'

'So does that mean *I've* got an otherhalf?' said Venk, looking puzzled, as Elliot printed out some pictures behind him. 'Because I'm pretty sure the world couldn't cope with that level of cool!'

'And you say it's all because of someone called "Scarmarsh"?' asked Clover, making her important face, and twiddling her fake moustache, seriously. 'How exciting!'

'Well, we mustn't get *too* excited,' said Alan, shifting his helmet up. 'Because that's how accidents happen.'

'He really *is* your opposite,' said Buster, nudging Alice.

'If we're right about all this, then we have to stop Scarmarsh before he zaps the King,' said Hamish, taking charge. 'If he zaps the King, then our Queen's had it.'

'I hate these evil bad guys and their awful plans!' said Clover, and Elliot stamped his foot in agreement. 'But what *is* his plan?'

It was a great question.

Hamish gave the signal to Holly. She whipped out a photo of King Les smiling in front of Buckingham Palace and the article from *Evil Icon* magazine. Then she unrolled a long piece of paper she'd prepared on the coach.

On it was written everything they thought they knew, and the words:

THE MEGAPOCALYPSE!
A plan in four stages by Axel Scarmarsh

Everyone shuddered as they read it.

'Okay,' said Holly. 'When we do drama at school, they say you have to get into character, right?'

Hamish shrugged. He hated drama. He didn't see the point in pretending to be trees or whatever. Whenever they asked him do it, he knew no one actually thought he was a tree. If they actually thought he was a tree, they must be mad. He really could not see how pretending to be a tree would help him in future life.

'So,' said Holly. 'To help you understand his plan, I am now going to "get into character" and pretend to be Scarmarsh.'

Everyone nodded, uncertainly. Buster got his torch out and shone it on her, like a spotlight. Holly closed her eyes for a moment and then suddenly opened them again and shouted: 'I AM AXEL SCARMARSH!'

'**Aaaargh!**' screamed Alan. 'It was Holly all along!'

'She's pretending!' said Alice, exasperated.

'**AND THIS IS MY PLAN!**' continued Holly. 'I call it
... the **MEGAPOCALYPSE!**'

Alan screamed again as Holly pointed at the unfurled paper.

MISSION:

To spread fear across every dimension
and become the first Evil Icon to rule
TWO WORLDS AT ONCE!

STAGE ONE:

BLANK ALL THE PEOPLE WHO ARE
MOST RESPECTED AND POWERFUL TO
STOP THEM INTERFERING!

STAGE TWO:

MAKE SURE MY POWER IS WITNESSED BY
AS MANY PEOPLE AS POSSIBLE!

STAGE THREE:

WHEN THEY SEE MY POWER, THEY WILL
GIVE IN TO ME!

STAGE FOUR:

RULE EVERYTHING,
GET NEW ROBES, BUY A BIGGER TELLY, ETC.

'Four stages?' said Elliot. 'Is that all? Are you sure there's not a secret fifth stage?'

'ZIP IT!' yelled Holly, with bulging eyes.

'I'm just saying,' said Elliot, with his hands up. 'There's usually a secret fifth stage. It's something to bear in mind!'

Holly nearly stopped pretending to be Scarmarsh, she was so annoyed, but managed to hold it together.

'The Queen is always tucked away inside the palace,' she spat, sinisterly, 'but the King will soon be on live TV in front of MILLIONS OF PEOPLE who will be terrified that I can get to anyone! *That* will be when I – Scarmarsh! – strike at the heart of TWO WORLDS AT ONCE!'

Holly stopped, dramatically. Everyone applauded.

'And after that,' said, Hamish, pale-faced, 'the world will bow down before him.'

'Well, we can't have that,' said Alice, and Alan agreed.

'No, you shouldn't bow,' he said, shaking his head. 'You should always bend from the knees.'

Elliot strode around, deeply concerned, with his arms crossed and one finger on his chin, thinking.

'If we go back to Otherearth,' said Clover, 'we'll need protection. Because what's to stop him from zapping us?'

It was a good point.

'He'll be looking out for us!' she continued. 'I mean – how did he even know you were in Otherearth?'

Hamish had wondered how those **MISSING KIDS** posters had got there too. Scarmarsh knew they were there. Had someone spotted them? Was that why he always felt like he was being watched?

Elliot looked like he'd had an idea.

'Here's what I don't understand,' he said, spinning round to face them. 'The King must have been on TV before, right? Scarmarsh must have had the chance to zap him in front of the world before now. So why has he waited?'

Hamish shrugged and shook his head. They'd all wondered why Scarmarsh was taking so long too, if that was his plan. I mean, King Les was always out and about. He loved being seen in public. You literally couldn't stop him trying to take selfies with tourists.

And not for them, for *him*!

'What if up until now there's been something protecting the King from the zap?' said Elliot. 'Something stopping Scarmarsh, that he knows won't stop him tomorrow?'

Everybody murmured, uncertainly.

'Look at these pictures,' said Elliot, spreading the photos he'd printed out across the table.

There was the Prime Minister, naked except for his pants.

There was the Sergeant Major, holding a cat called Mr Poopy.

There was Vapidia Sheen, unable to work out how to hold a pen.

And now there was Holly's picture of the King, standing in front of Buckingham Palace, his cheap tinfoil crown glinting in the sun.

'What one thing makes the King different from the others?' asked Elliot.

'Millions of pounds?' tried Venk.

'The palaces?' suggested Buster.

'His bottom?' said Clover.

Elliot paused. 'What?'

'He's got a weird bottom. It looks like a peach trapped in a sock.'

'No,' said Hamish, stepping forward. 'The *crown*. It's the crown!'

'Maybe Scarmarsh has tried to zap the King before now,' said Elliot, 'but the crown *deflects* the zap?'

'Yes!' said Holly, excited. 'That's why Scarmarsh is waiting for him to get a new one! Because he knows he'll have to take the old one off first! He's going to wait until the crown is off his head and the King is unprotected. Then he'll zap him in front of millions of people!'

They'd cracked it!

Outside, the gang rushed around. They had plenty to organise.

'We'll need food!' said Buster, sensibly.

'Kebabs!' said Alice, hopefully.

'Yes,' said Buster, humouring her, 'or in the morning I'll pop to Madame Cous Cous's International World of Treats and buy a multipack of Turkish Twizzlers and some Barcelona Banana Balls!'

The **PDF** was the only thing that could stop Scarmarsh now. Hamish was pleased they were back together.

They'd need Buster's technical know-how.

They'd need Elliot's unique genius.

They'd need Clover's mastery of disguises.

And they'd need Venk to . . . um . . . well, they'd find *something* for Venk to do.

Maybe he could hold their coats!

'**PDF!**' he shouted. 'Wheels rolling at 6 a.m! We need to travel to Otherearth, locate Scarmarsh, rescue the King – and *save the world!*'

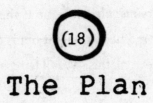

(18)

The Plan

Early the next morning, with notes for parents left on pillows, detailing monsters, parallel universes and how very important it is to always try and save the world, the **PDF** rocketed towards London in Buster's ice-cream van.

They looked a determined bunch.

They were all wearing fake moustaches and enormous hairy sideburns that Clover had passed around, as well as blue boiler suits Hamish had borrowed from Slackjaw's Motors. They'd rubbed oil on their faces to make them look more like grown-ups too.

Soon, they could see the city under grubby grey clouds. As usual, the first thing they could spot from the motorway was the huge BT Tower in the distance. It used to be called the Post Office Tower in the old days, and everyone agreed that was a much cooler name. A ring of dark cloud surrounded its peak. It jutted out of the ground, standing tall over all the other buildings for miles around.

Hamish felt nervous. He sat right at the back of the van and, in this quiet moment, thought of his dad.

Would he approve of this? Was Hamish doing the right thing?

Sometimes, it was as if he could feel his dad watching him. And, since his first conversation with Alex, every time he saw a blackbird he wondered if that was Dad, looking out for him. Except for the time he saw a blackbird poop on a bench. He didn't think his dad would do that.

But he couldn't help but wonder whether his dad would want him putting himself in danger. Mums and dads want their kids to stay safe. That's the whole point of being a mum or a dad. Those are the only instructions you're given.

But equally kids want their mums and dads to be safe. And that's what this was all about. Finding his dad. And stopping anybody else from getting zapped.

So yes, this had to be the right thing to do.

He wished he'd had the chance to ask Alex more questions. Next time he saw her he was going to grill her on exactly where his dad was. Thinking about his dad, he suddenly felt filled with something. Bravery? Confidence? He knew for sure now that his father hadn't just left him on Boxing Day. There had been a reason he'd had to go. And now Hamish was going to help him make it all worthwhile. He'd prove he was worth coming home for.

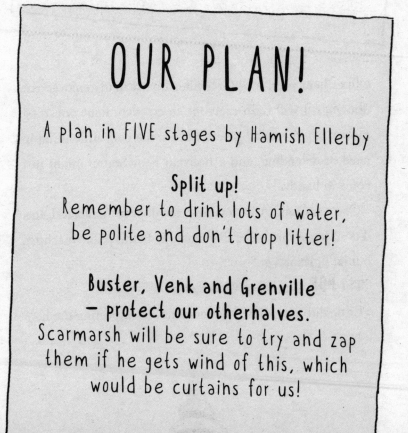

An hour or so later, as Buster parked up in the alley next to Arcadian Lane, Hamish got out one of his mum's Starkley Town Council clipboards.

'Everybody out!' he shouted, and pointed at what he'd drawn on the other side of Holly's MEGAPOCALYPSE presentation. 'I present *our* plan!'

OUR PLAN!

A plan in FIVE stages by Hamish Ellerby

Split up!
Remember to drink lots of water,
be polite and don't drop litter!

Buster, Venk and Grenville
— protect our otherhalves.
Scarmarsh will be sure to try and zap
them if he gets wind of this, which
would be curtains for us!

Wear plenty of tinfoil!

Clover — we will need a whole bunch of your super-great disguises so that we can blend in to polite society! Hamish and the others — **protect the King!**

Then we must see . . . to Scarmarsh!

'Excellent plan!' said Grenville. 'I particularly enjoyed the drawings. I will train everyone to do my unique wrestling moves. My otherhalf is sure to be some poor little thing in need of defending, and a Bolivian Foot Stamp might just come in handy.'

'Come on,' said Alice, opening the door to Arcadian Lane. 'I don't know how we're all going to fit in this photo machine, but let's give it a go!'

The **PDF** were off to Otherearth.

Little did they know, but someone was expecting them.

*

Two great circular clouds hovered over the city like a pair of giant eyeballs.

'**Coo-ee!**' said Grenville, impressed. 'Look at this place!'

The gang were standing under the big sign that read:

WELCOME TO LONDON
A CITY LIKE No OTHER!

The word **WELCOME** had been underlined *twelve* times now. (Though they knew the bit about it being 'a city like no other' wasn't *quite* true because, to be fair, it was quite a lot like *their* London.)

All around them, colourful taxis beeped cheerfully and people bustled. Most of the kids had never seen buildings as impressive as the ones in front of them. Everyone seemed very appreciative. Only Hamish remained quiet. Maybe he was being paranoid – or maybe it was just those massive clouds – but there was that eerie feeling again.

At least they were protected now. On the train, Elliot had handed everybody a small piece of tinfoil.

'Keep it near your head!' he said, as they began to walk through town. 'If I'm right, the foil should deflect anything

Scarmarsh tries to beam at us if he spots us!'

Alan had carefully plastered his over his helmet.

Clover had used hers as a scrunchie to tie her hair back.

Buster had twisted small pieces into his Afro, which made him look a bit like he had metal spikes, the way a robot hedgehog might.

'Look . . .' said Hamish, pointing up at a big screen as they reached Piccadilly Circus.

Friendly news headlines ran across the bottom.

+ + + + + + + + + + WOO-HOO! + + + + + + + + + + +
+ + + + + KING TO BE RECROWNED + + + + + + + + +
+ + + + + IN FANTASTIC CEREMONY TONIGHT!
+ + + + + THAT SHOULD BE QUITE GOOD!+ + + +

Above that, they were showing a repeat of the latest episode of *Question Me Sensibly*. Lots of important-looking people were simply dancing around in their underwear.

Now there was an interview with the Hungarian Prime Minister. He was staring at the camera, blank-eyed, while the subtitles underneath read: 'I LIKE TENNIS BALLS! TENNIS BALLS ARE ROUND! I LIKE ROUND THINGS!'

The kids walked on, with Hamish deep in thought.

'I think Scarmarsh must be upping the pace!' he said.

'Maybe it's because he knew we were in town yesterday!'

'Uh-oh,' said Venk, pointing.

There were more **MISSING KIDS** signs on lamp posts, complete with pictures of Hamish, Alice, Holly and Alan.

'Maybe it's time for proper disguises,' said Clover. 'Just in case he's still looking for us?'

The low growl of approaching vehicles filled the air.

A long line of enormous police vans had turned the corner and was now heading up the street. Six of them. Each was big and white, but a little scuffed and dirty. Even from this distance, the kids could see that they were full. But full of police officers?

Not exactly . . .

'Keep back,' said Hamish, pushing his friends into an alleyway. 'Stay hidden.'

And, as they crouched to keep low, the vans began to pass, one by one.

Inside each one they could make out the unmistakably sinister shape of *Terribles*, hiding under police helmets. Elliot began to tremble as he noticed one long, thin arm dangling casually from a window. It was pasty. And wet!

And seemed to have *dark brown mushrooms growing from the wrist*!

'The smell!' said Holly, as the vans all trundled by. 'Oh my gosh, the *smell!* It's worse than ever!'

'I think they're on the lookout for us!' said Hamish, horrified.

In that small alleyway just off the main road, Clover set her bag down.

Just beyond, a group of French schoolchildren sat outside the National Portrait Gallery, while a teacher stood in front of them giving them a lecture. If you listened closely, though, you could hear she was just saying, **'I am imagining an ice cream!'** over and over again while the children all sat there, making notes and looking confused.

Apparently, Scarmarsh was now targeting almost *any*

authority figure he could. It was like he was warming up for the evening's main event.

'Right!' said Clover. 'We need to blend in. So this is what I've brought.'

She emptied her disguise bag.

The kids all stared.

Among others, there was a bear costume.

A ballerina dress.

A clown suit...

'Hmm . . .' said Hamish. 'Clover, are you sure by blending in . . . we might not actually stand out even more? I mean . . . if I saw a clown walking down the road next to a ballerina, I might actually—'

'Shhhh!' said Alice, quickly, and with some horror.

Wandering past the end of the alleyway, she'd spotted a group of firemen and women slowly thrunkling by. But, to the trained eyes of the **PDF**, this wasn't a normal group of firemen and women. They were *huuuuuge*. And they had their helmets pulled right down low. They were gruntling and trumpling and scanning the streets with their squinting, beady eyes.

'They're everywhere!' said Holly, pulling the group to one side, to hide behind some bins.

'Their uniforms mean they're hiding in plain sight,' said Clover, impressed by the ingenuity of their enemies. 'It's brilliant!'

The gang cowered a little longer, as the dreadful beasts disappeared down the road.

'We need to get a move on,' said Hamish, realising that if they'd been spotted, that would have been Game Over. 'Buster – take Venk and Grenville and get to Sparkley sharpish.'

'Sparkley?! How?' asked Buster. 'We didn't bring the ice-cream van with us. And it's not like we can just ask a policeman for help!'

'Wait!' said Alice, reaching into her pocket and bringing out a small green business card. 'Maybe we *do* know someone who can give you a lift.'

'Yo-Yo?' said the lady in the taxi, pulling up to the payphone. She had enormous glasses and a little flat cap. 'Did somebody order a taxi cab by any chance?'

Hamish smiled. This quiet and polite woman seemed to drive the only *black* taxi in London. The ID on the window read **LEONA BANNISTER**.

'We're friends of . . . well, a sort of *relative* of yours,' said

Alice, smiling sweetly at her, trying to win her over. 'A gentleman called Leo.'

'Leo?' said Leona, confused. 'Sounds familiar. But I'm not sure I know a Leo.'

'Oh, you'd love him,' said Hamish. 'Drives a taxi. Hates his satnav.'

'Hates his satnav? Oh, I *adore* mine. Anyway, where are you going?'

Grenville piped up.

'Starkley,' he said. 'Britain's Fourth Most Boring Town!'

Leona looked uncertain. Leona looked like she was someone who was often uncertain. This was not a cab driver who'd passed her Gift of the Gab test.

'Do you mean Sparkley?' she said, timidly. 'On the coast? But I don't recognise the description—'

'To Sparkley!' interrupted Buster, flinging open the door for Venk. 'And step on it!'

As they were about to set off, Hamish tapped the window.

'Remember, Buster,' he said. 'Keep our otherhalves safe!'

Buster gave him a big thumbs up, as Leona's satnav said,

'Destination: Sparkley!'

'Good luck, H,' he said. 'And stay hidden!'

Saving the world seemed quite a big task, now that Hamish thought about it. Not only did it involve saving the King, but also stopping this Scarmarsh chap.

'I'm not sure this bear costume really suits me,' he said, struggling to keep his paws on. 'Plus, it's rather heavy.'

Clover had taken the ballerina outfit and appeared delighted, especially because she'd added another, bigger fake moustache to complete the look.

Elliot was a small cowboy.

Alice was a policeman.

Alan just stayed in his American football clothes, because he said polyester clown suits can often catch on fire.

Holly looked very annoyed she'd been left with the estate-agent costume.

'I'm very sorry, Clover,' she said, bringing out her pen. 'But you're going in the RevengePad for this.'

'People must think we look weird,' said Alice, frowning, as they passed a giant billboard with nothing but two huge eyes on it.

'It's not people we're worried about,' said Hamish, staring up at it, nervously. 'It's Scarmarsh and the Terribles. If they're looking for us, they're looking for kids. Not estate agents and ballerinas.'

'Hiding in plain sight!' said Elliot, clicking his spurs.

'Well done, Clover! Using his own trick against him.'

'Yes,' said Hamish, still not able to shake the feeling of being watched. 'But, if we're going to stop him, we need to know where he can be doing this from. How can he see so many people to zap them?'

They found their way to a small square with a park in the middle. It seemed like a pretty safe place to sit down and have a think for a bit. A sign said **FITZROVIA SQUARE** and they kneeled down on the grass together.

OtherLondon was a busy place. Even though it was pretty friendly, and everyone wearing a hat still tipped it and said hello, they all still had somewhere to be and something to do. They rushed around, not paying the world quite as much attention as they might have. No wonder the Terribles were having such an easy time of it.

Buses passed by.

A chopper whizzed across the sky.

The nearby giant Post Office Tower cast its shadow across the grass.

Hamish checked The Explorer, as in the distance Big Bertha's bell struck 2 p.m. In just over four hours, the King would be getting his new crown and, if they were right, Scarmarsh would strike. Time was of the essence.

'Hmm,' said Hamish, thinking. 'Maybe Scarmarsh is in a helicopter. Maybe that's how he sees everything everywhere?'

'No,' said Elliot. 'How would he zap people from a chopper? I don't think it would be steady enough for focused zapping.'

'Wait a minute,' said Alice. 'What if it's something to do with TV? I mean, the King is going to be on TV tonight, and the PM was on TV when it happened to him.'

'That's true,' said Elliot.

'And Vapidia Sheen's been zapped,' added Alice. 'And that weatherman. And remember how blank everyone looked as they stared up at the screens that day?'

'Do you remember the satellite trucks in Starkley?' said Clover, a thought striking her. 'Remember how huge they were? Well, aren't satellites a way of zapping and beaming and targeting and so on?'

Elliot clicked his fingers. 'Satellites!' he said.

'Does that mean Scarmarsh . . . is in space?' said Hamish, his heart sinking. That would explain why no one had seen him. And how he could see everybody.

Hamish looked up into the deep blue sky. He'd seen a whole show about satellites once – how they could spot even the smallest thing on Earth as they moved slowly and sinisterly through space. What if Scarmarsh was up there

171

right now? In the cosmos? Staring at him? He felt for the tinfoil in his collar, hoping it was enough to protect him.

Now they all looked up into the sky, feeling tiny and pathetic and hopeless – this bear, this cowboy, ballerina, policeman, American footballer and estate agent.

'Wait . . .' said Elliot, slowly, as he dropped his gaze ever so slightly and noticed something.

'What is it?' said Hamish, trying to see what Elliot was staring at.

'What if he's *not* in space?' said his friend, adjusting his glasses. 'I mean, it's a little inconvenient to be way up there when you're planning world domination.'

They all turned to look at him.

'But satellites are in space, aren't they?' said Hamish.

'Not all of them,' said Elliot, wisely, like he was really going to enjoy this.

'Then where is Scarmarsh hiding?' asked Alice.

'What if,' replied Elliot, dramatically, 'just like the Terribles, and just like *us* right now . . . Scarmarsh is **hiding in plain sight?**'

He raised his hand, and slowly pointed.

Sparkley

An hour and a bit after they'd set off, Buster, Venk and Grenville stood on the edge of Sparkley and stared, amazed.

Leona had driven them there in record time. It seemed satnavs really did work. Leo would be furious. She'd been absolutely appalled to hear about what Scarmarsh had been up to. She said she'd have to tell the other cabbies. And that would take courage – Leona liked to blend in. She didn't see the point in standing out. But, if the police and the fire service had been compromised, maybe London's taxi drivers would have to step up and help keep order. She'd fired up her satnav, spun the car round and shot straight back to the city to spread the word – gift of the gab or not!

The boys patted each other on the back. They had a mission of their own. And they were home . . . *sort* of.

But there was no boring beige town sign here.

No – this sign was huge, and all lit up in bright Hollywood lights.

And it was the only place name they'd ever seen that was so excited about itself that it ended in an exclamation mark.

Sparkley!

BRITAIN'S FOURTH MOST EXCITING PLACE!
Twinned with Las Vegas, Rio de Janeiro and the Moon!

'Whoa!' said Grenville. 'Look at this place! How come our otherhalves get to live in such an exciting place?'

'Because we got the boring one!' said Venk, flatly.

Once a year, a fairground was set up in Starkley. It was clear that in Sparkley it was only once a year that there *wouldn't* be a fair.

And what a fairground it was! Lights lit up the sky. The screams of delighted, faraway children filled the air as they were thrust into the air on Vertical Boosters or thrown for miles on the Sparkley Slingshot.

There was a stadium where the town's small bandstand normally was. From the posters, you could see that just about every rock star in the world was coming to Sparkley!

Bippy Lipswitch and the Tickle-me-pinks!

Baroness Flabbington!

Sonny Griffiths and his Ridiculous Yellow Ukulele.

The Elderly Brothers!

Venk studied the posters a little closer. The Elderly Brothers' eyes were blank.

'Let's explore,' he said.

The boys were in awe. Everything was the same – but different.

There was old Mrs Neate standing outside The King's Arms, smoking a pipe and patting a dog. Back in their world, *Mr* Neate was always trying to *kick* them!

Then there was Herr Fussbundler, sitting in his car listening to *Men's Hour* on the radio. They were interviewing the first male bishop, who was always trying to get people to singalong to boring 'hers' (which are a bit like hymns).

But, as they made it to the town square, the boys saw something that shocked them to the very core of their being.

'Oh my gosh,' said Buster, staggering backwards and reaching out for the others. 'No! How awful! How dreadful! This can't be allowed! This must be illegal!'

The others looked where he was pointing.

MONSIEUR COUS COUS'S
GALAXY OF HEALTHY PUNISHMENTS

Even Madame Cous Cous's International World of Treats was opposite in this world! Was nothing sacred?

'*Yeuch!*' said Buster, pointing at the window display. '*Health sweets!*'

'Asparagus lollies!' yelled Grenville, clutching his own head in horror.

'What are *they*?' said Venk.

'Just an asparagus on a stick!' said Grenville, in disbelief. 'And look – spinach gobstoppers! Broccoli gum! Kale creme eggs!'

'This is inhuman,' said Buster, shocked. 'We need to *save* these kids!'

'Where do you think they'll be?' asked Venk, looking around. 'Our otherhalves?'

'Hmm – if they're the opposite of us,' said Buster, frowning, 'where's the one place they'll *really* want to be right now?'

The boys thought about it then nodded at each other.

'*SCHOOL!*' they all said.

Where Could He Be?

Elliot's guess about where Scarmarsh was hiding out definitely had legs.

Do you know what he thought?

Well, let me tell you about the most secret and most secretive building in the whole of London.

Can you think where it might be?

Down in the tunnels?

There's a little place called Eel Pie Island – do you think it might be there?

Or underneath the River Thames, maybe?

Well, did you know that, until fairly recently, there was one building in London that the government decided should be . . .

TOP SECRET?

In fact, it was so Top Secret that it didn't even appear on any maps.

Even though you could stand right next to it and touch it!

177

And it was so Top Secret that even if all you did was accidentally happen to get it in the background of a photo you were taking of your Auntie Liz holding a whippet, then technically you were going against the Official Secrets Act!

That meant they could lock you up, shine a spotlight in your eyes and bark questions at you! And all because your auntie wanted her picture taken with a whippet.

And it was all the more strange because this was not a building that acted like it was a secret at all.

It was right there, bold as brass.

In fact, it still is.

Sometimes, to really rub in how visible it is, it glows at night, one red light blinking at the top of it.

Just like the Terribles, *this was a building hiding in plain sight*.

Isn't it amazing what you can see when you really look?

If Elliot was right, Scarmarsh's associates must have been delighted when they found it. I mean, there are plenty of places you could choose in London. There's even a sharp, spiky building called the Shard – and if that name isn't perfect for evil-doers to set up base in, I don't know what is.

So why wouldn't they have chosen this Top-Secret building to set up base in? Somewhere nowhere would see them, but from which they could see everybody? The one place everybody in the whole city could see, but that nobody was looking for?

Nobody apart from Elliot, that is.

'I think I've cracked it,' he said, still pointing.

'Cracked what?' said Alan, panicking, in case he meant a window or a rib.

'Cracked the problem,' said Elliot. 'I think I know where Scarmarsh is!'

The terrifically tall and slender Post Office Tower stretched far into the sky above them.

'It was built as a way of shooting beams all over the world,' said Elliot, excited, as they stared at it from the doorway of the place opposite. It was called Really Fried Chicken and it was filthy. 'You know – for telephone calls and things like that.'

'How about for TV shows?' asked Hamish, looking up at it. Now that Elliot mentioned it, there certainly did seem to be a lot of satellite dishes hanging from its side.

'Oh, yes!' said Elliot. 'Particularly for TV shows. Instead of putting cables everywhere like we do now, they just decided to build a really tall building so that they could beam their

rays everywhere. You can see everything from up there!'

'Everything?' asked Alice.

'You can see for miles. You can definitely see *every important building* in London and even further than that probably.'

'That's how they're doing it then?' said Holly. 'That's how they zap people?'

'Well,' said Elliot, 'maybe. We'd need to take a look. But the problem is, we can't see in the windows from down here. It's impossible! Look how high up they are!'

How could they get a peek inside the Tower?

'Whoa!' said Alan, frightened of falling, even though they were all still on the ground.

Outside the Tower, at the front doors, two tall and gangly figures crept about. They were wearing hard hats and bright yellow tabards. They were supposed to look like builders, but they were huge, hulking Terribles! One of them spun its head round to see if anyone was watching, then leaned down behind a car to lick the stinky brown liquid from its exhaust pipe ... then stood back up, a little dizzy but satisfied.

Uuuuurgh!

A milk float rolled up, and four more Terribles dressed as milkmen jumped out, carrying crates of bottles. Hamish began to realise why there seemed to be so many more milk floats in this world than in his. And whatever was in these bottles was not milk. These bottles were pure black.

Well, if there were Terribles here, that meant two things:

They had an interest in that huge Tower and that meant Elliot's guess was probably right.

The kids couldn't exactly stroll in and ask what on earth they were up to.

Then Hamish remembered something.

Something he'd seen when he and Alice had first arrived in London.

Something that could very well be the key to taking a closer look at that Tower.

A *much* closer look.

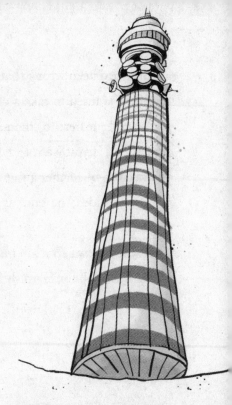

Jimmy had been wrong that Christmas. He'd told Hamish that if he wanted to take a closer look at things, he should just stand nearer to them. But Hamish thought that sometimes, if you want to take a closer look at something, you need to be further away.

'I have an idea,' he said, as he threw his bear costume to one side.

Because this wasn't a job for a bear.

This was a job for Hamish Ellerby.

And Then
There Were More

In Sparkley, Buster, Venk and Grenville crept through the gates and quietly peeped through the windows of Winterbourne School.

Inside Class 4E, a tall and vaguely familiar-looking woman was bounding round a classroom.

'Who's that?' wondered Venk.

But a sign on the door read:

MISS NEVER LONGBLATHER ALL-ACTION TEACHER!

'Never Longblather? She's certainly very energetic,' said Grenville, as through the open window he saw the teacher throw herself into a forward roll.

'And now!' shouted Miss Longblather. 'While you turn to page sixteen in your books – I will perform some Chinese Tumbling!'

All the kids smiled and turned to page sixteen, and Miss Longblather lit a small hoop on fire.

'Behold!' she shouted. **'The Ring of Doom!'**

'It's certainly a radically different approach to teaching,' said Grenville, as the boys moved to the next window. 'Maybe it's continental.'

'Hey,' said Venk. 'Check it out!'

He pointed at a girl in a red T-shirt who looked *remarkably* like Buster.

Lightly, Buster tapped on the window.

'*Psssst*,' he said, when she looked round, all big eyes and surprise. 'I'm you! You're me! Grab your pals. I have something to tell you!'

MEET THE ALTERNA-PDF!

NAME: BELLA

LIKES: Running, jumping and anything to do with exercise ever!

DISLIKES: Technology. Video games. Cars. Anything with an 'ON' button.

BELLA

VIOLET

NAME: VIOLET

LIKES: Long black-and-white documentaries about the history of wool.

DISLIKES: People who wear sunglasses indoors or who say things like 'Whatevs . . .' to try to be cool!

COLIN

NAME: COLIN

LIKES: Talking, although he often talks FAR TOO LOUDLY which doesn't help him blend in.

DISLIKES: *Trying* to blend in because he just can't, as there are so many things to trip over or knock over and sometimes he just can't stop sneezing.

ELAINE

NAME: ELAINE

LIKES: Asking the question 'Why?' all the time.

DISLIKES: Being told to stop asking the question 'Why?' all the time.

'But why?' said Elaine, all confused, after Buster had explained everything for a third and then a fourth time.

'Because Scarmarsh is trying to take over the world!' said Buster.

'But why?' said Elaine.

'So that he can control it!' said Buster, who was running out of ways to put this differently.

'But why?' said Elaine.

'Because he's evil!' said Buster.

'But why?' said Elaine.

'Because . . . he was born that way!'

'But why?' said Elaine.

'I wish your otherhalf Elliot was here to explain!' said Buster, exhausted.

'We need to protect you all,' said Venk, coolly. 'If they zap you, they zap us, and it's the same the other way round.'

The otherhalves had all taken the news quite well, considering how HUGE it was. And they were fascinated to find that there were others out there so similar and yet different to them. The one thing they didn't like, though, was that they were apparently 'Neverpeople'.

'Maybe *you're* the Neverpeople!' said Violet, stamping her foot, losing her cool.

'Chill out!' said Venk, who you could never accuse of losing his cool.

'Well, how come *we're* the Neverpeople?' said Violet. 'I find the idea very demeaning!'

'Calm down!' said Grenville, taking a step forward. 'There's another issue which is far more important!'

He studied the **Alterna-PDF** and made a very serious face.

'Where's *my* otherhalf?' he said, putting his hands on his hips.

The Sparkley kids looked a bit awkward.

'Because I need to find that little lady!' he said.

No one said anything.

'Look,' he said. 'If my opposite is the opposite of the daring Grenville Bile, aka *El Gamba*, then she will be a dainty little flower in need of some expert Bile protection. I am not being sexist, I am merely dealing in facts. She's my opposite, so she's probably quiet as a mouse. She will not be as smart as me, nor will she be as streetwise. She'll be weak and delicate, and probably always fainting. She'll . . . wait, what are you all looking at?'

Everyone else now seemed to be looking at something just above his head.

Something standing right behind him.

Something big.

Something tall.

Something that made a noise that sounded like . . .

'HULLOOOOO . . .'

Grenville's eyes bulged.

He turned, stunned, to see . . .

GRETA

NAME: **GRETA BILE** aka *Fem*ville Bile!

LIKES: Running. Hugging. School.

DISLIKES: Nose-picking. Bullying. Mexican wrestling. And books about funny tractors.

'Right, well, hello,' said Grenville, looking up at Greta, pretending his pride wasn't hurt. 'You, er, needn't worry. I'll look after you, madam.'

'You're so **CUTE**,' said Greta, leaning down and patting him on the head with a *thud-thud-thud*, which actually rather hurt. 'I could eat you up!'

'That's enough of that,' said Grenville, trying and failing to bat her enormous hand away. 'I'll have you know I am an expert Mexican wrestler.'

Greta opened her jacket. She had three medals pinned to the inside.

Ju-jitsu Gold Medal Winner.

Best Karate Kick Ever Award.

Most Improved Trampolinist.

'Greta can open tins with her hands and throw balls for miles,' said Elaine.

'So can I!' protested Grenville.

'*Pffft,*' said Violet. 'Everybody knows that boys can't throw properly.'

'How dare you!' said Grenville. 'That is an outdated childish stereotype!'

'Anyway,' said Elaine, 'you did the right thing coming here. She'll look after you.'

'I DO NOT NEED LOOKING AFTER!' yelled Grenville, looking up at Greta. **'I AM GRENVILLE BILE AND I AM HERE TO LOOK AFTER YOU!'**

'Listen to his funny little voice,' smiled Greta, picking him up and cradling him like a baby. 'You're like a little dolly!'

'Look,' said Buster, taking charge, as Grenville fumed. 'It's very important that we find a safe place for you to hide until the **PDF** can sort all this out. We need somewhere out of the way and a lot of tinfoil.'

Just then, a milk float roared past, blaring out loud rap music. An elderly man inside casually tossed milk bottles from his window. Each of them landed perfectly upright and without smashing on each doorstep on the street.

'*Whoa!*' said Grenville. 'Who's *that?*'

'That's Montgomery Crinkle,' said Violet, smiling.

'The very best milkman in the country!'

Buster checked out the milk float. Montgomery must have done some *incredible* work to make it go that fast. Poor old Margarine Crinkle's milk float was rubbish in comparison.

It gave Buster the beginnings of an idea.

'The thing I don't understand,' said Bella as the milkman skidded expertly round a corner, 'is that Holly and Alan are out there, in London, right?'

'Yes,' said Venk.

'And they're fighting to save the world with your friends Hamish, Alice, Clover and Elliot?' asked Colin.

'Yes,' said Venk.

'And this is all happening right *now*?' said Violet.

'Yes!' said Venk. 'Right now.'

Greta Bile took a step forward and shook her huge head.

'And you came here and expected us to **HIDE?'**

Let's Take
a Closer Look!

Hamish knew they had to work fast. It was already nearly 5 p.m.

Before they could stop Scarmarsh, they had to make absolutely certain they knew where he was.

'We need to get back to where we started,' he said, as they clambered on to a big red bus. It was a good job kids could travel free on buses here, or they wouldn't have any money left for Chomps.

'Back to where, Hamish?' said Alice.

'Back to Greenwich. That's where we first arrived in London.'

'Greenwich?' said Alice, sitting down on the top deck, right at the front. 'Where we saw that big boat?'

'The *Cutty Sark*!' said Elliot, excited. 'I've always wanted to see that!'

'We're not going to look at boats,' said Hamish.

'Phew,' said Alan. 'Because I've not brought my life jacket.'

'You have your *own life jacket*?' said Alice, amazed.

'Who *doesn't* have their own life jacket?' replied Alan.

On the streets all around them, crowds of people were noisily making their way to the Tower of London. They were chattering excitedly about the King's recrowning ceremony, and carrying flags to wave in celebration. In just a couple of hours, King Les the Second would be standing in the Parade Ground. Little did everyone know that the second he took his tinfoil crown off, he'd be zapped and the world would know Scarmarsh's power!

At Trafalgar Square, huge screens showed the preparations for the ceremony.

At Downing Street, the press were still standing outside, angrily demanding to know where the Prime Minister was. (She was inside, trying to play Jenga with her best friend, the tea cosy. It had been a long game because Captain Dullard didn't seem in much of a hurry to take its turn, nor did it seem to understand the rules, or, being a tea cosy, be able to speak, or move.)

More and more Neverpeople wandered up the streets from Buckingham Palace, laughing and joking, unaware that this was the day when everything would change forever.

Finally, the bus reached Greenwich.

'Where now?' asked Holly, confused, as Hamish dragged them off the bus and started to walk up the hill.

'To the Royal Observatory!' said Hamish, who'd kept his plan quiet just in case they were being watched. 'What we need is a huge telescope!'

The Royal Observatory sat at the top of a hill in a park, overlooking the River Thames.

Outside, Hamish checked his Explorer to see how much time they had left and noticed something unusual. It was glowing green, like just by being here it was gaining power. There was something magical about this place, and Hamish knew he must be on the right track.

'To get past the security guards inside and get to the telescopes, we'll need a distraction,' he said.

'Don't you worry about that,' said Holly. 'I'll provide a distraction, all right.' Hamish had always been quite a shy kid. But not Holly. She had always been the opposite of shy. She strode inside, determined. Hamish was really impressed. He'd never have been able to do that so confidently.

A moment later, two tubby security guards ran outside, screaming.

Holly was chasing them with a fire extinguisher in each hand. She was pretending they wouldn't stop squirting.

'I'm so sorry!' she shouted. 'I don't know how to stop squirting you!'

She totally did. But the guards would rather run than hang around and get even more soaked and splattered in gooey white extinguisher foam.

Hamish winked at the others, and they snuck inside.

HH

'Cooooool!' said Elliot, beaming.

Down a long and squeaky corridor, door after door after door led to the Observatory's biggest and best telescopes.

'Did you know,' he said, 'that the galaxies and the stars and everything we can see make up less than 5 per cent of the universe? I wonder what's in the other 95 per cent! Could be aliens. Or whole planets made from toast.'

'Right now, all I care about is what's in the Post Office Tower,' said Hamish. 'Which is the best telescope to use?'

They pushed open a door to find a sign that said ***Onion Dome – this way.***

'Onion Dome?' said Alice. 'That sounds like the worst theme park ever.'

'Wait,' said Elliot. 'I did a whole school project on space. I wasn't supposed to – I was supposed to be doing Sports Day. But I think that's where they keep the super ginormous telescope. The Great Equatorial Telescope. It's the biggest in the country. It's *ma-hoo-sive*.'

'Can we use it?' asked Hamish.

'No, it's only for looking into space. But it *does* have a viewing platform outside. We can stand there – and use one of *these*!'

Elliot pointed behind him at the gift shop.

And right in the middle of the shop was the telescope Hamish had always wanted.

A huge **Gia-tron BugEye 5000** in British Racing Green!

The kids lugged the enormous telescope right up the dozens of white metal stairs that led to the very top of the Onion Dome.

'Remember,' said Hamish, 'when we open this dome, we'll be outside again and exposed. Make sure you're wearing your tinfoil in case Scarmarsh tries to zap us.'

Everyone checked that their foil was in place, and then Clover pressed the huge red button marked **OPEN**.

The whole dome started to vibrate as the roof above them began to part.

JUD-JUD-JUD-JUD-JUDDER

The roof opened and the kids clambered over the rails and on to the viewing platform above, all the while lugging the **Gia-tron BugEye 5000** on their shoulders.

Elliot got to work setting it up as the kids looked out over the city. In the distance, they could see more and more people heading to the Tower of London. In the sky above them, the Blue Arrows flew by in their amazing fighter jets, getting ready to put on a terrific display to congratulate the King.

'Okay, we're good to go!' said Elliot, flipping the lens cap off.

Hamish stood at the viewfinder, took a deep breath and peered through.

Sadly, it wasn't pointing at the Post Office Tower yet, so all he saw was a naked old man getting changed through a bedroom window somewhere in Finchley.

'*Yeuch!*' he shouted.

'Sorry!' said Elliot, moving the telescope. 'How's this?'

Now all Hamish saw was a baboon in London Zoo licking its own bottom.

'Elliot, this is horrible!'

'How about now?' said Elliot, panicking, and shifting the telescope further to the right.

'Yes!' said Hamish. 'That's it! That's the Post Office Tower!'

He was looking at the ground floor. Those Terribles from earlier were standing by another car, licking the juice from its exhaust pipe again. But at least it was pointing the right way now.

So Hamish moved the telescope up . . .

And up . . .

And up . . .

Past the bland concrete base . . .

Past the first windows . . .

Past the satellite dishes . . .

Up . . .

Up . . .

UP even faster . . .

And . . .

'Oh, no,' said Hamish, the blood draining from his face.

'What is it?' asked Clover, trying to inch past him to take a look.

'Oh, dear, no!'

23

I Wish We Hadn't Taken a Closer Look!

What Hamish saw through the windows of the top floor of the Post Office Tower chilled him to the core of the middle of the centre of his very bones.

He did not see Scarmarsh, that much was true.

But he did see something else.

Something that *proved* Scarmarsh had to be there.

What *were* those huge, awful, clanking, boxy things?

With rivets and nuts and bolts in their arms?

With stark, glowing eyes and sleek, smooth helmets?

Were they machines? Were they demons? Were they . . . *machi-mons*?

'They're Hypnobots!' said Holly, who'd just returned and put down her fire extinguishers, which were now completely empty. 'Oh, no! I read about them when I was in the British Library. There was an article in *Evil Icons* magazine!'

'What did it say?' asked Hamish, peeking meekly through the viewfinder again.

'They were just supposed to be a rumour!' said Holly.

But there they were, visible through the giant telescope, clear as day – and clearly not a rumour!

HYPNOBOTS!

Holly thought back to the article she'd read. At the bottom there'd been this:

LATEST FROM FRYKT

'Watch Out' for
Hypnobots! p.16

Did you spot it too? And FRYKT – *wasn't that Scarmarsh's base*? Holly thought it was. So, over a can of Cherry Coke and a butternut flapjack, she'd read the article . . .

Word reaches us that there may or may not be more going on on the island of FRYKT than we first thought!

'We have developed a range of foolproof, terrifying watching devices,' an unnamed spokesman said, evilly. 'Meaning we can watch almost anyone, almost anywhere, at almost any time...! We will tell people this is for their own good and is in fact protecting them. But we will know that really it is "Project Hypnobot" ... an interesting rumour indeed!

EVIL ICONS MAGAZINE VOL XX ISSUE X

Well, it wasn't a rumour any more. This was how Scarmarsh could see everybody all the time!

Hamish was right to be horrified at the idea of Hypnobots. They were awful.

Do you know what they were?

They were giant, metallic black robots!

CLANKING! CLUNKING! THUMPING when they moved!

Blue pulses of light shooting around their bodies every few seconds. Able to sit perfectly, hypnotically still for hours on end. Each one staring and glaring out at another part of the pitiful city below it.

You couldn't reason with a Hypnobot. You couldn't convince one you were nice, or that they should stop watching you. They didn't care if they scared you. They were emotionless.

They never slept, or blinked, or shut their eyes.

Those dark eyes were like camera lenses, always on, always shifting focus to see what they could spot next.

Hypnobots could see *anything* with those evil peepers. They could zoom right in at a hundred miles an hour. They could scan the city from left to right. They were always ready to spy on whatever they'd been told to with those huge, round black eyes with piercing blue lights. That was why they needed to be so high up – so they could stay vigilant.

And when they spotted their target?

BVVVVVT – an arm is raised.
BADOINK – a button is pressed.
WAAAAAAAH! – an alarm sounds.
KAPOOOOOOW! – the zap

shoots out, ready to blank another poor soul and their unwitting otherhalf.

Oh, you might think you can just hide down an alleyway. Or stay indoors. But all the Hypnobots needed was a brief appearance near a window. Or a momentary reflection in a shop door or car wing mirror. They saw *everything*.

Hamish shivered. No wonder he'd always felt like someone was watching him. They *had* been! But why hadn't the Hypnobots zapped him the first time he'd come to Otherearth? They'd known he was here because someone had put those signs up.

'It gets worse,' said Holly. 'The article said they can also be used . . . in battle.'

'Oh, great,' said Elliot, covering his eyes with his hands. 'Battle robots. Why not?'

'How big are they?' asked Alan, innocently. 'Can I see?'

'What does it matter how big they are?' said Alice. 'They're battle robots!'

'HAMISH!' yelled Alice, peeking through the telescope. 'I think something's happening!'

She let him have the viewfinder, and immediately he saw what had scared her.

The enormous eyes of an awful Hypnobot were flashing and whirring! There were four little holes in its forehead, and now steam was whistling right out of them, like when a kettle boils.

What did that mean? Did that mean it was about to strike?

Hamish could see that the other Hypnobots were going crazy too, madly flailing their arms up and down and screaming and steaming too.

'It's pointing at something on the streets below!' said Hamish, and the others all gasped. Alan nearly fainted.

BVVVVVT – Hamish watched as the Hypnobot raised a huge arm.

BADOINK – now it slammed a button with such force that the windows in front of it seemed to shake.

A satellite on the side of the Tower began to tremble and turn.

'It's going to zap someone!' said Hamish, horrified.

'Who?' yelled Holly. 'Where?!'

KAPOOOOOOW!

Hamish yanked the telescope round to follow the direction of the zap as it tore through the sky, rippling the air behind it.

On a road far down below, a poor, innocent police sergeant was giving directions to two American tourists outside a museum.

ZAAAAAAAP!

The sergeant fizzed and vibrated!

His two little feet levitated off the ground for a moment!

His helmet spun round on his head!

His shoelaces went all straight and pointy!

Two wisps of smoke curled out of his ears as he landed softly on the street again!

Then he started just stroking the tourists' confused faces and blowing wet raspberries at them.

'That's no way to welcome people to the country!' yelled Hamish, furious.

He pointed the telescope quickly back up to the Tower.

The Hypnobot was cackling and crackling while its Hypnopals tried to high-five it with their huge metal hands.

One of them started pretending to blow raspberries for a laugh, and spat nuts and bolts all over the room, which just annoyed everybody.

A giant black **BACK TO WORK!** sign suddenly blasted on behind them and they fell silent, their evil eyes whirring and turning again like all-seeing, all-knowing camera lenses.

'They're so powerful,' said Hamish, quietly.

'But we can beat them, right?' said Holly, nudging him. 'Right, Hamish?'

'Battle robots,' he said, slowly, and then Hamish Ellerby sighed. 'I think that's it, guys. I think we're done.'

'What do you mean "done"?' asked Holly because Holly would never give up. 'Don't make me put you in my RevengePad, Hamish!'

'We've done all we can on our own. We've found Scarmarsh and his Hypnobots. We know he's guarded by Terribles and that the city is crawling with them. It's time to tell the grown-ups. We need to alert the army.'

'Aside from the fact that grown-ups are always useless in situations with battle robots, there's a big problem with your plan,' said Alice, and Holly seemed pleased *someone* wanted to fight. 'We met the chief of the army at Downing Street,

remember? The Sergeant Major had been zapped. He was just going on about having a cat called Mr Poopy. That means both he and his otherhalf have gone blank!'

'Then we tell whoever is second-in-command,' tried Hamish.

'What if *they've* been zapped too?' said Holly, desperately.

'Then we tell his *third*-in-command!' said Hamish. 'Or we tell someone who's still got some power!'

But everyone knew that, at the rate Scarmarsh was going, the only person left in a position of power would probably be the deputy assistant regional manager of a shoe shop, or something.

'The point is,' said Hamish, 'we can't do this on our own. We're kids. But if there aren't any grown-ups in power then they can't do anything either.'

The gang were silent. It really did seem like all was lost.

But then . . .

'Wait!' said Alice. 'There *is* someone!'

Hamish blinked. Who?

'Someone who's been right in the middle of this, but who's stayed unzapped!' said Alice. 'Someone who could take charge and alert the army! Someone we've met but overlooked!'

Hamish had no idea who she could be talking about.

'Mysterio!' she said.

'What – that Romanian guy?' said Elliot. 'But we're on Otherearth and he's back in our world!'

'It's just like Leo and Leona – if you can get through to his otherhalf, you can explain everything. And Mysterio's otherhalf will definitely want everything back to normal! She can look in the Prime Minister's address book and find a number for the most important person in the army!'

It was the only idea they had.

'Fine,' said Hamish, fishing out the business card Mysterio had given him back in Starkley the night the PM had been zapped. 'I'll call "Mrs" Mysterio. You keep your eye on the Tower. And stay hidden!'

Down below, there was a payphone. Hamish scrambled down a drainpipe and then reached for the receiver, popped some coins in the slot and dialled the number.

The line was strange and crackly. It didn't sound like a normal ringtone.

BVVVVVVVOOOOOBBBBT

Hamish waited for the call to be answered. How was he going to explain this? How was he going to convince Mysterio's otherhalf?'

'HALLO?'

'Erm . . . is that . . . Mysterio?' said Hamish, sheepishly.

'This is . . . she,' replied the voice, which soundly oddly familiar as well as just . . . well . . . odd.

'My name is Hamish Ellerby,' said Hamish. 'This will sound crazy, but—'

'HAYYYMEEEESH,' said the voice. 'Think godness you'se okay!'

What? How did *this* Mysterio know who Hamish was?

'I knows all aboot what you've been doing. *Alex* told meee.'

Alex! So Alex had had the same idea and found someone in Downing Street who could help! Thank goodness for Alex!

'Phew!' said Hamish, so glad he'd found a friend on Otherearth. 'But listen – we need to hurry.'

'Hurry?'

'You need to get the whole army to the Post Office Tower right now!'

Hamish looked up at his friends, relieved, and gave a little thumbs up. It was all going to be okay!

'The Post Office Tower?' said Mysterio, mysteriously. 'Why the Post Office Tower?'

'Because that's where Scarmarsh is,' said Hamish.

Mysterio went quiet. Then . . .

'You *know* where Scarmarsh is?'

'Yes, and you need to send helicopters because there are Terribles at the bottom, and you need to be prepared for battle robots who'll probably see you coming on account of them being Hypnobots.'

'Hypnobots?' said Mysterio.

'They're the worst,' said Hamish. 'They're huge, and terrifying, and steam comes out of their foreheads, and—'

'Where are you, Hamish? Can you see the Tower from where you are?'

'Yes,' said Hamish. 'I'm looking at it right now.'

'Right now? Well, you must be close to it,' said Mysterio. 'If you can see those "Hypnobots"?'

Hamish noticed the tip of the Tower start to glow red in the distance.

'Just the opposite actually,' said Hamish. 'But I'd better not say too much because I bet they can trace calls too, but let's just say we've been "scoping" the place out . . .'

Hamish could hear something now. Was that an alarm sounding? Somewhere far away?

'That's very interesting,' said Mysterio, and Hamish couldn't help but notice that Mysterio's voice wasn't quite as foreign as before. That was weird – if the normal Mysterio was foreign, wouldn't his Otherhalf be too?

'Hamish!' called Holly, urgently. She was still looking through the telescope, up on the viewing platform.

'So can you help?' Hamish asked, as from somewhere behind him a ship's bell rang.

'I can certainly help,' said Mysterio. 'But, if you could tell me exactly where you are, I could send someone to pick you up? To keep you safe?'

'HAMISH!' called Holly again.

This time, Hamish covered the receiver and mouthed, 'What *is* it?'

Holly pointed at the Tower.

All sorts of lights were flashing on it now. The middle section had started to revolve. Bright white beams of light shone from its tip and spun round London like spotlights across a prison yard. Vast satellite dishes began to creak and move. This wasn't like before, when they'd zapped the police sergeant. This was something *bigger*.

'I can't say any more, I have to go!' said Hamish, hanging up the phone and running back to the drainpipe to hoick himself up again.

'What's happening, Holly? What's wrong?' he said,

clambering over the wall and running to the viewfinder.

But he could see for himself now. The satellite dishes were surrounded by those angry red flashing lights. Terribles were pressed up against the windows of the Tower, scanning the streets around them.

He moved the telescope up a little and saw . . .

OH MY GOODNESS.

A Hypnobot!

Staring straight *back at him!*

The giant metal beast's eyes burnt yellow and seemed to widen for a second as its lenses spun round, zooming in on Hamish and his pals.

THEY KNEW.

And they were ANGRY.

'It's too late!' yelled Hamish. 'They know we're here!'

'Let me see!' said Alan, trying to get round him.

'What do we do?' shouted Alice.

'I don't know!' yelled Hamish. 'I think we run!'

'I want to see!' shrieked Alan.

But, as Hamish stepped to one side and Alan bent down to take a look, his helmet stopped him from getting close enough to the telescope. He began to desperately fiddle with the strap.

'I say we call Leona,' said Holly. 'Get her to drive us out of here.'

'Elliot,' said Hamish. 'Mysterio's sending the army, but we need to get to the King! What's the quickest way to the Tower of London?'

'We run to the river!' said Elliot.

'Good!'

'Then it's a short walk to catch the 188 bus.'

'Less good,' said Alice.

'Then it's a brisk sixteen-minute walk, another bus and hey presto – we're there in less than an hour and a half! Unless it rains and they cancel the buses.'

'There *has* to be a *faster* way,' said Hamish, who turned to look at the huge bright red Tower one more time before seeing something that horrified him. 'Alan – what are you *doing*?!'

Alan had loosened the strap of his helmet and was now taking it off.

'I want to look in the viewfinder!' he said. 'I'm scared and I want to see what's happening!'

'DON'T TAKE YOUR HELMET OFF, ALAN!' screamed Alice.

But Alan flung it to one side, forgetting for just that moment and in all this excitement that on that helmet was the tinfoil that was keeping him safe.

'ALAN!' screamed Alice. ***'NOOOO!'***

ZAAAAAAAP!

A bright white pulse of light frizzed through the air and popped around Alan like a bubble. His hair blew up into the air and stood on end for a second before relaxing very slowly and going back into position. His fingers straightened and his feet tingled and he may or may not have quickly and quietly farted.

Everyone clasped their hands to their mouths.

(Because they were horrified – not because of Alan's windypops.)

Was that – a *zap*?

'Alan?' said Hamish. 'Alan – are you okay?'

Alan turned to Hamish and smiled.

Maybe he was okay!

'Imagine if you could poop chewing gum,' he said, very quietly.

Oh, no! They'd got Alan!

Unless that was just something he was genuinely thinking?

'Imagine if you could **POOP CHEWING GUM!**' he said again, giggling.

No – he'd definitely been got!

And wait – if they'd got Alan, then *that* meant . . .

'ALICE!' said Hamish.

He rushed to his best friend and spun her round.

She had a wide grin on her face, but Hamish looked deep into her eyes.

He knew he could tell from her eyes.

And Alice's eyes . . . were *blank*.

'No – please,' said Hamish, starting to panic. 'No, Alice, anyone but you!'

'Always be prepared,' said Alice, quietly, blankly. 'Always be prepared.'

The air around them started to get cooler, the sky greyer. In the distance, Hamish could hear the mighty cheers of distant Terribles carried on a rising wind, as they celebrated this small victory, and it filled him with cold rage.

'Alice – snap out of it! Please!' said Hamish, shaking her shoulders, as alarms around the city began to ring and ring and **RING**.

'She's gone,' said Holly, placing a hand on his arm. 'Scarmarsh zapped Alice and Alan.'

Hamish could not believe it.

Not Alice Shepherd.

His fists tightened and his brow furrowed. What would he

do without Alice? How could Scarmarsh have *done* this to her?

'They're coming!' said Elliot, who'd taken over the telescope. 'The Hypnobots have sent the Terribles! *Hundreds* of them!'

On the roads, for miles around, vans were turning in the streets as the robots spread the word.

Police cars, builders' lorries, ambulances . . . they were all now headed right this way.

A strange black fog of diesel fumes and Terrible-stink began to carpet the roads of London, as Hamish put on his most determined face yet.

'We need to get Alice and Alan out of here!' he said. 'We need to get to the King – this can't all be for nothing!'

'But how, Hamish?' asked Holly, looking desperate. 'They're coming and we're trapped up this hill! We'd need a miracle to get out of this one!'

Which is when Hamish turned round.

Driving up the hill at some speed was a very unusual vehicle indeed.

24

Think Quick, Hamish!

'The Terribles!' screamed Clover, terrified, pointing at what was headed their way. 'They're here!'

It certainly seemed like their luck was up, what with two of them zapped, and the rest about to be taken away by the Terribles themselves.

'Do we have any weapons?' asked Hamish, hopelessly.

'I saw a toilet plunger inside?,' suggested Elliot.

The strange little vehicle was getting closer. Hamish took a deep breath.

So this was the end of the adventure.

But ...

BEEP BEEP!

Hang on. What *was* that?

BEEP BEEP BEEEEEEP!

'Is that ... a *milk float*?!' said Clover.

It skidded to a halt in front of them.

'Hi, gang!' said Buster, leaping out.

But wait – that wasn't Buster!

That was *Bella*!

'Our otherhalves?!' shouted Elliot, delighted.

In the back, where all the bottles would normally be, sat the **Alterna-PDF**. For a blissful moment, everyone just stared at each other in wonder.

'Which one of you is my otherhalf?' said Elaine, pushing her glasses up her nose, as she stepped out and stood next to Elliot, who pushed his glasses up his nose.

It was pretty obvious, to be honest.

'There's no time for introductions now!' said Hamish, snapping out of it. 'We need to get to the Tower of London!'

'We can drive from here,' said Buster.

'No we can't,' replied Hamish. 'The Terribles are coming. We'll have to try and avoid the roads.'

'Well, what are we going to do – fly?' bellowed Greta Bile, who was clutching Grenville like a teddy bear. He looked extremely annoyed by this.

Think, Hamish! Think!

Could they get to a Ghost Station? Or should they just stay put and hide?

Hamish looked down the hill.

Wait.

No – they couldn't.

Could they?

It was worth a try!

'Everyone back in the milk float!' he yelled.

The kids bounced down the hill in the milk float while the first of the Terribles were still heading up on the roads around them.

'They're almost at the Observatory!' shrieked Elliot, horrified.

'Imagine if you could poop chewing gum,' said Alan, nudging Greta. He really didn't seem to grasp the gravity of the situation.

'I made a few modifications to Mr Crinkle's float!' shouted Buster, with his foot slammed down on the accelerator and the milk float **GROWLING** away. 'Mrs Slackjaw let me use her garage! It's even more powerful now!'

'I am not comfortable with this!' shouted Bella, who always said that if something wasn't broken, you shouldn't fix it.

But look! At the top of the hill, the great beasts were covering the Royal Observatory like a gas, spreading out, screeching, flipping over cars as they sniffed where the kids had just been. Their telescope was flung high in the air.

'There!' yelled Hamish, pointing. 'Head for the *Cutty Sark*!'

'That big boat?' replied Buster. 'But it's nowhere near the water!'

Buster was right. The *Cutty Sark* was just a tourist attraction these days. It hadn't sailed in forever. It had been mounted high in the air, held by thick glass panes, which sort of looked like water underneath it and reflected the sun.

The float skidded to a halt by the famous old clipper ship, leaving tyre marks on the concrete behind it.

'Buster – do you think the float is powerful enough to pull the *Cutty Sark* into the river?' Hamish asked.

'Oh, you wouldn't believe what I can make her do,' said Buster, revving the engine.

'My worry is the ship!' yelled Bella, worried. 'It's like a million years old!'

Buster pressed a button and a big silver winch dropped from the rear of the float.

'Hook that to the front of the ship!' he shouted, and the gang leapt into action. Buster was terrible at tying, so Elliot and Clover attached it to the ship's hull in a double knot.

'Okay, Buster! **DO IT!**'

Buster revved the milk float – BVVVVVVVVVVVVT!

'Get on board the ship!' yelled Hamish. 'Everybody!'

BVVVVVVVVVVVT!

'It's not working!' said Clover. 'How can this possibly work?'

'Have faith,' said Holly, calmly, as Buster revved again.

BVVVVVVVVVVVT!

'More, Buster!' yelled Hamish, as Holly dragged a blank-eyed Alice and Alan on board. 'Give it everything she's got!'

'PUUUULL!' shouted Clover. *'PUUUULLLL!!!!!'*

The old ship began to creak and strain.

'They've spotted us!' yelled Buster. 'Look!'

At the top of the hill, a Terrible was **ROARING** to the others, and pointing one awful finger at them. A group of monsters began to pound towards them on all fours.

'Keep going, Buster!' yelled Hamish, as the others clambered on board.

Now the glass around the bottom of the boat began to splinter and crack.

'It's working! It's working!'

Buster jammed his foot on the pedal with everything that little float had. Its wheels began to spin. The rubber was burning. Sparks were flying.

BVVVVVVVVVVT!

But it was no good! Despite Buster's best efforts, the little milk float just wasn't quite powerful enough.

'LET ME HELP!' yelled Greta Bile, rolling up her sleeves and plucking Grenville from where he stood. **'GIVE ME A HAND, LITTLE MAN!'**

The first of the Terribles was now not far away. Saliva flung round its mouth as it galloped ever closer.

Greta and Grenville ran round the back of the old boat and began to push ... and **PUSH** ... and **PUSH!**

'NNNNNgggggggghhhh!' grunted Greta.

Then ...

CRACK!
CRACK!
CRACK!

The glass began to splinter and shatter even more! Thanks to Greta and the milk float, the *Cutty Sark* broke free from its surroundings ...

BANG!

Its hull slammed down on to the concrete as tourists screamed and ran. The back of the ship was now raised high into the air, with Greta and Grenville hanging on for dear life ...

BVVVVVVVVT! went the float, wheels still spinning, but it was working! The tyres had fallen apart now, flinging burnt rubber everywhere, but it was pulling the *Cutty Sark* towards the water!

The ship reached the concrete slide.

'Just a bit further, Buster!' yelled Hamish, as the first Terrible made it to the rear of the boat . . . It jumped up, tried to catch the back of Grenville's heels with its scampering paws, but slipped . . .

Buster rocketed forward, taking the milk float right into the water. Black smoke poured from behind him, the giant *Cutty Sark* now **SMASHING** and **SPLASHING** into the water behind it. It bobbed for a second as it righted itself . . .

'SAILS!' screamed Hamish. 'NOW!'

UP went the sails, catching the wind in a split second and puffing out with a FAFFAF! as ugly new Terribles leapt and desperately jumped to try and catch the boat.

The *Cutty Sark* began to move away from the riverbank . . .

'We did it!' shouted Hamish, delighted, and with the biggest grin in the world. 'Holly – raise the Union Jack!'

'The *what*?' said Holly.

'The Union Jack!' said Hamish. 'The flag!'

'Ohhh,' said Holly. 'In our world we call it the Union *Jill*!'

And as the Union Jill was hoisted upwards, and the sails caught another welcome burst of wind, Hamish felt victorious.

But wait!

Oh, no!

Down there, on the milk float, still in the water!

'Buster!' shouted Hamish. 'Why aren't you on board?!'

But Buster was having trouble.

He and Bella were standing on the roof of the milk float as the engine *put-put-putt*ed its dying gasps.

And the problem with floats is . . . *they don't float*.

It was sinking, with both kids still on it!

Hundreds of Terribles now lined the shore, jumping up and down and grabbing at a boat they couldn't reach.

'They're staying put,' said Venk, confused.

'They hate the water, remember?' said Hamish. 'Now we need to turn this boat around to get Buster!'

But Buster knew what had to happen.

'Go!' he shouted, bravely. 'If you come back, they'll get us *all*!'

He stood, bobbing, on top of the slowly sinking milk float, as 200 awful monsters now calmly stared at him, smiling sickening smiles. Puddles of Terrible drool formed at their clawed feet and slickered down into the river, coating it in a thin grey gel.

Hamish didn't know what to do.

So he did the only thing he could.

Buster and Bella looked smaller and smaller and smaller as the *Cutty Sark* sailed away.

25

Sail of the Century!

'We can't just leave them there,' said Clover, as the *Cutty Sark* sailed down the Thames at quite a clip. 'What will the Terribles do to them?'

'We have to,' said Hamish, the wind in his hair. 'Buster was right. We have to get to the Tower in the next half an hour to stop the King from being zapped. If we go back now, they'll catch us all and that would mean the end of the world.'

But Hamish felt terrible. And sad. And confused. And very guilty.

He felt responsible for Alice and Alan being zapped. And, if it hadn't been for him, Buster and his otherhalf would still have been back in their homes, probably perfectly safe and eating hot dogs or talking to flies.

This was a disaster. Two **PDF** blanked. Two **PDF** captured.

But, as the ship broke through the waves, and Hamish felt the water spatter his face, he also felt determined.

Whoever this Scarmarsh chap was, he had to be stopped. It didn't help that Hamish couldn't visualise him. He'd never seen him, which made it harder to work out how they were going to beat him. Or his army of Terribles. Or his all-seeing Hypnobots.

Hamish turned to see that what remained of the **PDF** was just standing, staring at their **Alterna-PDF** counterparts.

No one really knew what to say to each other. It was like when one classroom of kids meets another one entirely and everyone goes a bit quiet and shy.

'Okay, we're all quite different,' said Hamish, gently. 'But, if we're going to save the King and stop Scarmarsh, we have to work together as a team. Just remember this – we always thought we were complete people. But really we were always just half of something. Now that we're together – we're finally whole.'

He made his best 'inspiring' face. But no one looked inspired. It was just a bit awkward.

Colin was staring at Clover, who still had her fake moustache on. Colin kept bumping into things and knocking stuff over. Clover didn't think he'd be very good at spying.

Violet was staring at Venk, wondering why he always felt

the need to take sunglasses everywhere.

Grenville looked grumpy as he kept trying to stop Greta from combing his hair like he was a doll.

Elliot kept trying to explain what was going on to Elaine, but without being insulting I think it's fair to say she wasn't quite the genius he was.

'Scarmarsh is beaming these zap signals from very high up, you see,' he explained.

'Why?' asked Elaine.

'Well, because signals fly through the air.'

'Why?' asked Elaine.

'Because they need to get where they're going,' said Elliot.

'Why?' asked Elaine.

'Because modern construction techniques mean some buildings block signals.'

'Why?'

'Because old buildings used to be made of generally weaker materials.'

'Why?' said Elaine.

'Because people only had access to straw,' said Elliot, sighing.

'Why?'

'Because straw is a crop which is easy to grow.'

'Why?'

'Because straw makes up almost half the yield of all cereal crops worldwide.'

'Why?'

'Because ... because **IT JUST DOES** and **STOP SAYING "WHY?"!**'

There was a pause while Elliot calmed down. He was relieved that conversation was over.

Hamish looked out at the riverside. He couldn't see any Terribles. It seemed like they were safe. For now.

And then Elaine said, 'Why?' and Elliot nearly exploded.

'Because asking *why* won't change anything!' he said, going red.

'Why?'

'Because asking why to everything I say is confusing matters!'

'Why?'

'Because one is a question and one is a scientific fact!'

'Why?'

'Because a scientific fact is an answer!'

'Why?'

'Because **I DEAL IN ANSWERS** while

YOU seem to deal in **QUESTIONS** like *why why why why why?* and it's driving me *nutso!*'

Hamish knew they couldn't go on like this. How could a team work as a team if they weren't a team? He had no idea how to fix this.

'Hmmmmm,' said Holly, crouching down, and noticing a sign. 'Look where we're sitting.'

The little old sign said 'Poop Deck'.

The Poop Deck was the highest deck on the ship.

But still . . . what a name to give it.

'Haha,' said Venk. 'The Poop Deck.'

They all started to smile.

Holly looked at Hamish and winked and he realised what she was doing. Holly had noticed the same problem about the kids needing to get along, but she seemed to understand people in a way that Hamish didn't.

'The Poop Deck,' said Holly again, this time with a cheeky smile.

And then Colin said 'the Poop Deck!' and nudged Clover and they both laughed a bit more. Even Violet sniggered.

And then, out of the blue, Alan said, 'Imagine if you could poop *chewing gum!*'

And everyone started to laugh some more because sometimes the more you say a word, the funnier it becomes.

'I hope the army is on its way to the Post Office Tower,' said Hamish, joining in, 'and the chief brings Mr *Poopy!*'

And that was when they all began to roll around laughing and slapping the floor in hysterics.

Poop!

Only Alice and Alan sat still, a vague smile playing on their faces.

Oh and Elliot too, because he was actually a bit annoyed at all this childish laughter, especially when you consider the term 'Poop Deck' originates from the French word for 'stern', *la poupe*, which comes from the Latin *puppis* and – when you think of it that way – is really not very funny at all.

But Hamish knew why they were laughing.

It was sheer, delightful relief.

Relief that they'd escaped. Relief that they'd got this far.

And it was also *fear*.

Have you ever been totally told off by a terrifying teacher, and all you could do was laugh? You didn't want to, and you knew it was wrong, but that's all you could do, wasn't it?

Well, imagine that feeling – but multiply it by a thousand

monsters, one evil icon and the idea that the fate of all
humanity rests on your bony shoulders.

Somehow, this laughter had been bonding. This gang of
misfits and oddballs was finally beginning to feel like a team.

Spinning the Captain's wheel, Greta Bile leaned the *Cutty
Sark* round to the left so that they could go round a bend in
the river. She did this with one hand, while using her other
hand to slap Grenville's hand away from his nose.

'Look!' said Hamish, as they rounded another quick bend to
the right. 'Tower Bridge!'

It was one of London's most famous landmarks.

Right on the other side of it was the grand, ancient and enormous Tower of London – where final preparations for the recrowning ceremony would be coming to an end. All along the riverfront, Hamish could see people carrying Union Jills and heading for the fun.

As they sailed closer, the men and women who raise and lower the bridge began to panic and check their schedules. Why was the *Cutty Sark* coming at them so quickly?! Actually – why was the *Cutty Sark* coming at them at all?!

They stopped all the traffic on the bridge and jammed their fingers on the button marked '**RAISE**'.

Tourists and locals applauded as they watched the beautiful *Cutty Sark* splashing and cutting through the choppy waters and under the opening bridge, spraying water across the bow and looking magnificent.

'We're here!' said Hamish, as Greta threw a rope to shore and **heeeeeeaved** the great boat to a stop with her not inconsiderable muscles. 'But remember – we have to assume Scarmarsh is watching!'

Hamish caught sight of the words painted on the river wall just in front of the Tower and shuddered.

ENTRY TO THE TRAITORS' GATE

'Long live the King,' said Holly, high-fiving Hamish and jumping from the ship.

Let's hope so, thought Hamish, as he jumped after her, and into the unknown.

26

To the
Tower of London!

The Tower of London looked beautiful.

They'd really pushed the boat out this time.

There were flags everywhere. Red, white and blue bunting was draped across every gate and wall. Burly Beefeaters stood guard on each corner, holding pikes, tall axes and boar spears. Some were having their photos taken with excited Spanish tourists. A Pearly King and Queen held silver serving dishes with prawn rings and Wotsits on them, just in case anyone fancied a prawn or Wotsit.

This place had been a palace, a fortress and a prison over the years. It was home to the Crown jewels and legend had it that the Tower was protected by the jet-black ravens of London – the fierce, noisy birds with sharp beaks and scratchy feet. People always said that if the ravens ever left the Tower of London, it would fall. Once, it was also home to the Royal Mint, where all the country's coins were made, and it had also been the official Royal Observatory for a short while.

And did you know that for over 600 years it was a type of zoo?

But today it was to be where King Les the Second got his fancy new crown.

The kids stood just outside the main gate and Elliot shared a clever plan he'd been working on as they sailed down the river.

He thought they needed to scale the wall, drop down, hide in the bushes, fashion some basic weaponry out of twigs and sticks, slice through the seals of a window, pop the glass out, forward roll inside, eat a sandwich and then come up with a second, better plan.

'We need to be really super secretive,' he said, and everyone nodded because all this sounded properly excellent.

'Why?' asked Elaine.

Oh, not this again.

'Because we can't be seen,' replied Elliot, grumpily.

'Why?' asked Elaine.

'Because, if we're seen, they'll stop us,' he said, sighing.

'Why?' asked Elaine.

'Because we don't have tickets and we're not supposed to be in there!' said Elliot, now rather exhausted and finding having an otherhalf really quite frustrating. 'So let's get on with it!'

He tried to start scaling the wall, but he wasn't wearing the right shoes and just kept slipping.

'Wait,' said Holly. 'Elaine's right.'

'What?' said Elliot. 'All she did was ask why!'

'Yes,' said Holly. 'But sometimes you *need* to ask why, to make sure you know you know what you think you know, you know? Or no?'

Everyone looked a bit confused by that statement, except for Elliot who just laughed.

'But surely we know we don't have tickets and we're not allowed in!' he said, certain he was right. They couldn't exactly just stroll into the Tower of London without tickets to see the King, could they?

Elaine pointed at a sign behind him.

STROLL IN!
NO TICKETS NEEDED!
COME AND SEE THE KING!

'Oh,' said Elliot, a bit crestfallen. 'Yes, that seems like a lot less effort than my way. Well done, Elaine.'

So in they walked, bold as brass, joining the growing throng of people. But Hamish felt uneasy. He touched his collar to make sure his tinfoil was still there, then strained to see if he could see the Post Office Tower.

What he saw worried him. The tall, slender building was glowing bright red again.

'Must be in celebration of the King!' said an old lady to his left. 'Ain't that nice?'

Hamish scanned the skies. He'd been quite clear to Mysterio on the phone that the army needed to move quickly and he couldn't see any helicopters whatsoever. Maybe they were biding their time. Surely they had to strike soon? Unless Mysterio had been *zapped* and couldn't pass the message on?

Hamish felt his wrist suddenly vibrate, which was weird. He didn't normally have a vibrating wrist. It was The Explorer. He was surprised to see that it was glowing red too. The hands were spinning madly round, and then stopped, suddenly – both of them pointing straight at the Post Office Tower. It was a warning. It must be. He'd had no idea his dad's watch could do this stuff. What was it trying to say?

Hamish wondered whether Scarmarsh might be preparing to do some extra-strong zapping. He must have wondered how most of the kids had stayed immune from being blanked and the obvious thing to do would be to try harder. Hamish decided that maybe they should stay hidden – and they'd need extra protection while they were at it.

'Clover,' he said, having the beginnings of an idea. 'I've got a top-secret covert mission for you and Colin.'

Right in the middle of the Tower of London – just near the Parade Ground where in ten minutes the King himself would be standing – was the White Tower. They kept some pretty special stuff in there. Hamish had seen as much on the big maps they put up everywhere.

Clover and Colin snuck in through the old wooden door while no one was looking.

'Come on,' whispered Clover, who'd given a fake moustache to Colin and was talking very quietly. 'Up here!'

They started to pad up the stairs.

KABLANG!

'SORRY!' yelled Colin, who'd knocked a big metal dish off a window sill.

'Shhhhh!' said Clover, with her finger to her lips.

'SORRY!' he yelled again, trying to pick up the dish, but knocking it right down the stairs.

KABLANG CRASH **KABLANG!**

'Quietly!' whispered Clover, grabbing him and pulling him up the steps behind her. But he caught his foot on the top step and his shoe came off.

'MY SHOE!' he yelled.

'*SHUT UP!*' whispered Clover, who now realised this was becoming the least covert of all the covert missions she'd ever been on.

Colin kneeled down to pick up his shoe, but bopped his head on the bannister.

THUNK.

'OW!' he yelled.

'Ssshuuuussssh!' went Clover, now quite pink, because her otherhalf was the worst spy ever.

Colin took a step back, rubbing his forehead, but forgot

the stairs were there. He started to fall backwards so grabbed a curtain to stop himself, but it couldn't hold his weight and the whole lot came tumbling down with a **FWUMP**. A giant curtain rod clattered to the ground after it and then **CLANK CLANK CLANKED** all the way down the stairs.

Clover and Colin stared at each other.

Still – they were here. The Tudor Room.

'WOW!' said Colin, before catching himself and whispering. '*I mean – wow!*'

Right in front of them was exactly what they needed.

Outside, Venk and Violet had been scoping out exactly where the King would be standing when he got his new crown. Venk lent Violet his sunglasses and she felt pretty cool. In return, she promised to lend him a brilliant 3000-page book called *An Illustrated History of Wool*. Venk tried to fake a smile, but pulled a face that looked more like he had gas.

Around them, everyone seemed super excited that they'd actually get to see King Les in the flesh. The place was packed.

Deep in the crowds, Grenville and Greta had been keeping an eye out for the Terribles. They knew they wouldn't try and come in near the river. All those Terribles would most likely still be on their way back from Greenwich, using the roads. That gave the kids at least twenty minutes, they reckoned.

Hamish and Holly had placed Alan and Alice on a bench at the back where they'd be safe.

'Always be prepared,' said Alice, quietly, and Hamish gave her face a little stroke.

'If there is a way of bringing you back, Alice,' he promised, 'I'll find it.'

'Imagine if you could poop chewing gum,' said Alan, softly.

'Yeah, you too, Alan,' said Hamish.

'So what's the plan?' said Holly, clapping her hands together, ready for action.

And then the crowd of Neverpeople began to roar, as King Les the Second walked out of King's House and across Tower Green, waving happily, with absolutely no idea of the terrible danger that was just moments away.

27

Crowning Glory

As King Les walked on to the stage, Hamish felt incredibly nervous.

There were TV cameras everywhere. Some were on cranes, swooping around the place. If Scarmarsh managed to zap the King, it would be on televisions all over the world. From Barcelona to Brooklyn. From Bonnybridge to Bolivia. Everyone would know that Scarmarsh could get to *anyone* in *any* world. King. Queen. Whoever he chose!

The Post Office Tower looked like it was almost rumbling now. Like it was warming up for something. Hamish couldn't help but speculate why.

'I think Scarmarsh is making the zaps stronger,' he said. 'My Explorer is going crazy! Just like it did at the Observatory before a zap came our way. I'm not sure our tinfoil will be enough this time.'

'How long do we have?' asked Holly. 'The King's already on the stage!'

'MY PEOPLE!' shouted King Les into the microphone, and the crowd cheered and waved their flags. 'TODAY I WILL TAKE A NEW CROWN!'

'Oh my gosh,' said Holly. 'I don't think we've much time!'

'BUT FIRST,' shouted the King, clearly pleased to have a captive audience, 'I WOULD LIKE TO PERFORM A LITTLE CLOSE-UP MAGIC!'

He pulled a pack of cards out of his cloak. A few people at the back groaned. King Les thought he was a terrific magician. But cards tricks aren't much fun to watch from fifty metres away when you can't see the cards.

'Guys!' shouted Clover, peeking out of the door of the White Tower. 'Come quickly!'

The kids ran up the stairs. Colin had just knocked over a priceless vase and was sweeping it under the carpet. Clover was back in the Tudor Room and had everything ready.

'These should fit!' she said, pointing at a long line of amazing ancient suits of armour. 'Grab a helmet and a suit if you can!'

*

'AND FOR MY NEXT TRICK,' yelled King Les, loving the attention, 'I WILL COUNT TO ONE HUNDRED IN TAGALOG – THE NATIONAL LANGUAGE

OF THE PHILIPPINES!'

King Les was very proud of this. He cleared his throat and waited for silence.

'*ISA!*' he began. '*DALAWA! TATLO ...*'

The crowd started to shift uncomfortably. This was shaping up to be rather a long night.

'*APAT! LIMA! ANIM!*'

🐓

'I have to be honest,' said Elliot, clanking out of the door of the White Tower. 'These suits chafe in places I'd rather weren't chafed.'

'Always be prepared,' said Hamish, thinking of Alice and fixing his helmet to his head while sliding up the visor. 'Just look at the Post Office Tower!'

Its rumble had become a full-on vibration. If a building could look like it was revving up, this one was. Hamish noticed clouds of dust forming outside the windows, as the very joints and rivets of the Tower shook.

'The satellite dishes!' said Holly, whose suit of armour had brilliant ~~turqoise tarquise~~ *aquamarine* spikes all over it. 'The Hypnobots must be turning them!'

It was horribly, horribly true. Each and every satellite dish was now pointing straight at where the King was standing.

253

'OH!' said King Les, suddenly not counting any more and looking frustrated. 'I'VE LOST MY PLACE! HANG ON, LET ME START AGAIN!'

'It's about to happen,' said Hamish. 'We need to get close to the King. But how are we going to get through all these Neverpeople?'

It seemed impossible. There were grown-ups everywhere, all staring at the stage.

'I've got an idea!' said Clover, and she turned to Colin. 'Colin – try and sneak through the audience without anyone noticing.'

'**WHAT?**' said Colin, confused, and a bit too loudly.

'Try and walk through the crowd without anyone realising you're there!'

Hamish looked worried, but Clover winked at him. Colin shrugged and set off, disappearing into the crowd.

'OW!' shouted a woman, immediately, as Colin stepped on her foot with his big suit-of-armour boots on.

'OUCH!' shouted someone else, now hopping about and clutching their shoe.

'**SORRY!**' yelled Colin, accidentally stamping on to yet another set of toes.

'MY FOOOT!' screamed an old man.

'SORRY!' yelled Colin. **'I'M TRYING TO SNEAK THROUGH WITHOUT ANYONE NOTICING!'**

The crowd grew restless. What was this commotion? The King could sense people weren't listening to him any more.

'HELP!' yelled a lady, whose coat had now somehow caught fire. How did Colin do this stuff? The lady screamed and threw the coat in the air. People panicked. The TV cameras spun round to film the coat, instead of the King.

'HEY!' yelled the King. 'YOU SHOULD BE FILMING ME! I'M ABOUT TO DO FIFTEEN MINUTES OF GERBIL IMPRESSIONS!'

People were starting to run now. Flags were hurled in the air. This was the most brilliant distraction ever and it was all thanks to clumsy Colin!

'Every weakness is a strength!' smiled Clover, and Hamish cast another glance at Scarmarsh's base. It was almost shaking now, like the whole building was furious. Scarmarsh must be watching the TV. He knew they weren't filming the King. His big plan was at risk if no one could see it happening!

'He's going to do it now,' said Hamish, pushing through what was left of the crowd.

'RIGHT!' shouted the King. 'STAY WHERE YOU ARE! WE'LL DO THE CROWNING NOW! COME BACK, ALL OF YOU!'

And he gestured at one of his royal sidekicks, who stepped forward with the new crown resting on a giant purple cushion.

'KING LES!' shouted Hamish, trying desperately to get closer. 'DON'T TAKE YOUR CROWN OFF!'

'HAHA!' replied King Les, straining to see who'd shouted this. 'VERY FUNNY, BUT IT'S A CROWNING CEREMONY, SO I HAVE TO!'

He sat down on a special golden throne, ready to replace his crown.

'QUICKLY!' shouted the King, waving one imperious hand. 'LET'S DO THIS!'

Hamish was now just metres away. He reached the stage and tried to clamber up. A sidekick kneeled down, offering the King his new crown.

'BY THE POWERS INVESTED IN ME AS ME!' yelled Les, as the cameras found him again. 'I HEREBY AWARD MYSELF THIS NEW CROWN!'

He reached up to take his old crown off . . . when . . .

BOOOM!

A huge zap shot out of the Tower like a sonic wave. It tore up the air behind it, making the clouds in the sky look all wobbly from the sheer power.

The air sparked with electricity.

Everyone's hair rose from their heads.

A bright white light fizzed and sparked around the grand old Tower of London as the zap shot through the air.

Hamish *leapt* towards the stage . . .

28

Save the King!

'WHAT ARE YOU DOING, YOU MASSIVE NUMPTY!?!' screamed King Les the Second, after realising a ten-year-old boy in a 'borrowed' suit of armour had sent him tumbling to the floor.

As the crowds ran around and slapped into each other in blind panic, Hamish had taken the full force of Scarmarsh's extra-powerful **ZAP**.

His whole body was vibrating in his suit of armour, which was making a very high-pitched whine – the same sort of noise that happens when you rub the top of a thin glass. Hamish's teeth chattered and his fingers tingled – but he hadn't been blanked. The suit of armour had deflected the evil beam.

The King had been mere microseconds away from taking his crown off when Hamish had leapt. He'd shoved it straight back on the King's head. But he'd done it with such force that it had gone right over his ears and was now hanging round his neck like a fancy dog collar.

Alarms in the Tower of London were going off. Beefeaters ran for the King and surrounded him, poking their pikes up in the air, not sure where this invisible attack was coming from.

'Your Majesty!' said Hamish, his ears still ringing. 'You need to get out of here! A man named Scarmarsh is trying to turn you into a halfwit!'

'Oh, no!' said a Beefeater. 'He must have succeeded!'

Another Beefeater slapped her forehead. 'Yes!' she said. 'Years ago! When he was a baby!'

The King looked at them and raised his eyebrows.

'He may be a little slow,' said Hamish, 'but the King still has both his wits about him. But Scarmarsh will keep trying. He's got terrifying Hypnobots watching our every move and shooting rays from the Post Office Tower. Your neck-crown should protect you for now, King Les, but I've got a feeling that he's going to make his rays even *more* powerful!'

The King looked at the Post Office Tower. It was now *really* shaking, like an angry fist!

'Well, how do we get out of here?' he said, nervously. 'And where do we go?!'

'Hamish!' shouted Grenville, panting as he arrived, even

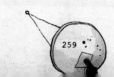

though he'd only run about ten metres. 'I think the Terribles are coming!'

In the distance, they could hear screaming. Half a mile away, an empty car was suddenly flipped into the air, high above the buildings. Who could do that but Terribles? They were more furious than ever. Particularly because it was rush hour, and you know what that's like.

How could they get the King out of here?

'Yo-YO!' came a cry from the gates. It was Leona Bannister! She was standing in front of a huge, long line of very colourful London taxis. 'Anyone need a lift?'

Leona had made good on her word and brought as many taxi drivers as she could. The other cabbies had taken a bit of convincing, but she'd done it. She'd found her gift of the gab! And Scarmarsh would never suspect a thing. *London taxis*, thought Hamish, *can hide in plain sight!*

'Leona!' said Hamish, quickly coming up with a plan. 'We need to get the King to Buckingham Palace at once. Scarmarsh will keep trying to zap him, and he's getting more and more powerful!'

'Then we need to hide which taxi the King gets in!' said Leona. 'That way he won't know which one to zap!'

But how could they hide the King?

'Clover – do you have any more disguises?' asked Hamish.

'We've used them all!' she replied, shaking her head.

Which is when something absolutely amazing happened. As if on cue, and as if they had planned it, the Guardians of the Tower – the six famous ravens – appeared from the Broad Arrow Tower and CAAAAAAAAWED in the air.

CAAAAAAAAAAW!
CAAAAAAAAAAAW!

The ravens of the Tower of London flew and swooped and cawed, and soon, from the river, the sky began to *fill* with ravens . . .

And crows! And blackbirds! And jackdaws! And rooks!

The **FAF-FAF-FAF-FAF** of their wings was deafening. Litter blew from bins and danced in the air. Dust swirled. The sky darkened under their coal-black feathers, as this cloud of birds blocked the light.

'They're hiding us!' said Hamish. 'The Hypnobots won't be able to spot us!'

'But how did they know what to do?' said Holly. 'They're birds!'

Hamish knew how.

Belasko.

The Basque word for raven.

This was his dad's work. Somehow, his dad was helping them. They weren't alone!

'Get the King in the cab!' shouted Hamish, and Holly pulled Les from the stage and shoved him into Leona's taxi. 'Take him to Buckingham Palace!'

Hamish and Holly watched as the rest of the **PDF** jumped into the cab with the King. Leona fired up the ignition and then got on the radio.

'All right, girls!' she said, as it crackled to life.

'And *boys*,' said a grumpy voice on the radio. 'It's Jeff here and it would be nice to feel included sometimes.'

Leona sighed.

'All right, girls *and Jeff*,' she said. 'You know the plan!'

'Hang on,' said the King from the back seat, suddenly realising something. 'What do you mean, I may be a bit slow?'

'GO!' shouted Hamish.

And, under the shifting cover of hundreds of birds, the taxis roared into life, filling the streets and then peeling off, one by one. Down alleys they whizzed, across roads, round and round and round roundabouts. Scarmarsh wouldn't know which one had the King in it!

But he wasn't going to let that stop him trying.

Hamish and Holly watched from the turrets of the Tower of London as Scarmarsh sent out **ZAPS** in ever-wilder directions. He was clearly panicking.

ZAP!

ZAP!
ZAP!

Cars fizzed and glowed as the beams hit, but Leona still shot through, hurtling across Tower Bridge and hitting a sharp right on Druid Street. Her satnav tried to tell her she was crazy and that she should really slow down, so she threw it out of the window. Leo would be proud.

Scarmarsh shot more zaps out all over London.

ZAP!

It missed and hit a cat.

ZAP!

It missed and zapped a pop star.

ZAP!

It missed and blanked a pigeon.

ZAP! ZAP! ZAP!

Faces in the retreating crowds turned blank in an instant as eyes widened and brains went 'boof!' People stopped dead in their tracks and just stared.

'The King will be safe at Buckingham Palace,' said Hamish, watching in horror as these wild zaps fizzed and sparked in the skies above London.

'What about us?' said Holly. 'What do we do now?'

'Now?' said Hamish, looking out over the city, then turning to face his new friend. 'Now we take the fight to Scarmarsh.'

29

It's Him!

Hamish and Holly Ellerby had been extra-specially careful.

They were heading straight into the lion's den. Right into enemy territory. Straight . . .

To the Post Office Tower.

Hamish knew the only way to stop Scarmarsh was to get close to him. The army should be there by now, and Hamish could fill them in on everything that had been going on.

The streets of London had been trashed by rampaging Terribles on the hunt for the King. Cars had been overturned. Windows smashed. A bin was on fire.

Even though they were sure Scarmarsh was too busy to be on the lookout for them, the two kids used alleyways and back roads to make their way ever closer to their enemy.

Finally, they found themselves at the foot of the great Tower.

There were far fewer Terribles guarding it than there had been before. Hamish had a dreadful feeling they were all heading to Buckingham Palace, furious the kids had given them the runaround. Maybe it had been a mistake to tell the King to go there. Hamish just thought that, like most of us, he'd be safest at home.

And, worse still, the army hadn't turned up yet. Now would be the ideal time to invade the Tower. Where were the soldiers? Where were the battering rams? Why was no one doing any abseiling or parachuting?

It was just them. Just Hamish and Holly.

Hamish thought sadly of Alice. The time to act was now, but could he do this without her?

As they hid back in the doorway of Really Fried Chicken, Holly counted all the Terribles she could see.

'There's one walking round the bottom of the building dressed as a window cleaner,' she said. 'There are two dressed as security guards in the lobby. There's one *reeeeally* fearsome ugly one pretending to be a traffic warden.'

She looked a bit closer.

'Actually, I think that's just a traffic warden. The point is this is going to be tricky. How are we going to get inside and make it to the top?'

Hamish tapped his chin. He wished Buster was here. Buster would come up with something ingenious. He'd rig the lifts to shoot them straight to the top. Or he'd make the automatic doors to the Tower go crazy so that they locked the Terribles out. If they had to get inside, Buster would have known how.

And then Hamish spotted that first Terrible again.

'Actually,' he said, 'maybe there's another way.'

On the outside of the Post Office Tower, if you look really closely, are some very special rails. They were put there when the Tower was first built, even though they were hardly ever used these days.

They were put there for window cleaners.

'Put these on,' said Hamish, handing Holly some blue overalls. 'And this hat!'

They were standing on the tiny outdoor cradle that hoisted window cleaners all the way up the tower. Hamish thought this would be the perfect way to get to the top. You've heard of thinking outside the box? This was thinking outside the Tower. And, if they were disguised as window cleaners, maybe the Terribles would just assume *they* were Terribles too.

Holly looked uncertain. She stared at the buttons marked **UP** and **DOWN**.

'Hamish . . . I'm not great with heights,' she said.

'What?' said Hamish, but of course that made complete sense. Hamish loved heights. He couldn't get enough of rollercoasters like the Gap-toothed Otter or the SpindleMonkey when the fair came to Starkley. 'Holly, be brave.'

'Someone once lifted me on to their shoulders when I was a toddler,' she said. 'I hate heights so much I put them straight in the RevengePad.'

'You had a RevengePad when you were a *toddler*?' said Hamish. 'Holly, you've got to learn to let some things go!'

'If I come up there with you,' she replied, ignoring this, 'do you really think we can stop Scarmarsh? Do you think we can find out where your dad is? And . . . and my mum?'

Hamish put a hand on her shoulder.

'Things only happen if you try,' he said, wisely. 'I'd rather try and fail than be too scared to try at all.'

Holly took a deep breath, nodded to herself, then slammed her small fist on the button marked **UP**.

᚛᚜

As the platform shuddered and rose, and Holly grabbed on to the rails for dear life, Hamish pulled his hard hat down low. He tried to whistle because he imagined window cleaners usually whistled, but he couldn't remember any tunes, so it just sounded weird. Holly and Hamish attempted to act casual as they passed the first long line of windows.

They held their breath.

Inside, they could see dozens of belching, bilious Terribles in what resembled a telephone exchange. They sat at desks in front of what looked like a million wires. Some of them were listening in on telephone calls and making notes with their slippery, slimy fingers. But none of them looked up at the two little window cleaners.

The platform rose higher. This was where the Tower really began. They passed sign after sign on level after level.

HIGH-VELOCITY VENTILATION MACHINES

TRANSMISSION APPARATUS ROOM

Holly's grip on the rails tightened. This cradle did not seem secure.

Every now and again, they'd see another Terrible, dressed as a security guard or telephone engineer, wandering down a corridor, snuffling and gruntling along.

AERIAL GALLERIES

MICROWAVE TRANSMITTER ROOMS

They were getting higher and higher. Holly didn't dare look around. But, if she had, she'd have seen a beautiful sight. All of London beneath her. The British Museum. Westminster Abbey. Battersea Power Station. *Everything*.

'Look!' said Hamish, suddenly, because inside a room, right at the back and completely surrounded by Terribles, were ...

'Buster and Bella!' said Holly, breathlessly. 'They're safe!'

Their two friends were sitting on chairs in a room marked **ZAP CONTROL** with no possible escape. But at least they were there! At least they were okay!

'Scarmarsh must be trying to get information from them,' said Hamish.

The cradle kept climbing upwards, every now and again jolting and frightening them.

Now they were more than halfway to the top and it was getting windier. They were at the vast satellite dishes that would turn and target the Neverpeople.

'Scarmarsh must be at the very tip,' said Hamish, as the old cradle caught the wind for a second and swayed, turning Holly's face a bit green. They were nearly 150 metres in the air!

On they went, the cradle creaking as they reached the next set of windows, to reveal ...

Terribles sitting right at the window, glugging down their dinners ...

Rotten apples!

Filth stew!

And black milk! (Which was called 'blilk' because that's exactly the noise you make after drinking some.)

Hamish had never seen a Terrible eat close up before. It was the most disgusting, diabolical sight. Food spattered the window as they squelched their bright yellow teeth into it, spraying the room with huge globules of out-of-date food juice. But the Terribles were so engrossed in their grossness that they didn't look up as the cradle passed by.

'Check it out,' said Holly. 'This bit is rotating!'

It was true. As they approached the next section of the Tower, they could see it slowly revolving.

'Careful,' said Hamish. 'Pretend you're washing windows ... because I think this might be ...'

THE HYPNOBOTS!

There they were, in all their enormous, clanking, camera-eyed glory! Staring soullessly out over the city.

For a moment, the kids were absolutely certain they were done for. How could these Hypnobots fail to see them? They were right there!

But the robots seemed to look past them. They were so used to searching in the distance that they couldn't see what was right in front of their noses. And of course they were focused on finding the King. Hamish followed their eyeline, and with a sinking heart saw that they were staring at Buckingham Palace. Had they sent their friends straight to the most obvious place possible? Had that been a mistake?

'Don't move a muscle,' said Hamish. 'We're still going up!'

Now they were approaching the very peak of the Tower. Can you imagine how high up that was? Can you imagine how Holly's tummy felt? It was so windy up there, and the cradle creaked and cracked and swayed from left to right.

But they had to keep going. They had to!

And, right at the very top, the cradle jolted to a stop.

'This is it,' said Hamish. 'This is where we get off.'

There was a small, thin walkway for them to balance on, with a safety railing in case they needed it. And, at the end of the walkway, one small window had been left slightly open.

Slowly, very carefully, they stepped on to the walkway.

'Don't look down,' said Hamish, which immediately made Holly look down. She started to shiver and tremble. One wrong move and she was toast!

'I'm here,' said Hamish. 'Remember – you're half me. And I'm half you. And together we're whole.'

'I can't do it, Hamish,' she said.

'If half of you can do it,' said Hamish, 'then you're halfway there!'

Holly nodded, bravely, as Hamish opened the window further. He peeked inside. There were dozens of framed photographs from around the world.

There was the TV tower in Berlin.

The Tokyo Skytree.

The Stratosphere Tower in Las Vegas.

Frankfurt's Europa Tower.

A tower in Auckland. Moscow. Sydney. Kiev.

'There are towers everywhere,' said Hamish, understanding something. 'All over the world, all of them hiding in plain sight! London is just the start. Scarmarsh's plans may be bigger and badder than we ever thought.'

The two kids lifted themselves up through the window and tumbled into a room.

They were safe!

Until the moment, of course, that they realised they weren't.

There was the smell, for a start.

A Terrible smell.

Then there was the drool coating the floor, slickery and

slimy, and nearly three centimetres thick.

There were the snarls and breaths and grunts.

And there were the boots, standing in the goo.

Two shiny black boots, directly in front of Hamish's face.

'*GOT YOU!*' said Axel Scarmarsh, grabbing both children by the scruff of their neck, and, as he *yanked* them up to eye level, Hamish could not believe his eyes.

The Battle of Buck House

Hamish Ellerby was struggling to take it all in.

He had met Axel Scarmarsh before.

'YOU!' said Hamish, as a drooling Terrible tied him to a chair and double-checked the knots. 'But . . . but why?!'

'Why what?' said Scarmarsh, scowling. 'Why am I doing it? Or why was I pretending to be . . .' He smiled and paused theatrically. **'*MYSTERIO?*'**

It was him! The Prime Minister's 'adviser'!

The accent was gone, and with it the strange purple suit.

Hamish now realised exactly why the army had never turned up to take back the Tower. He'd trusted Mysterio to pass on the message when the very person he was trusting was the person he was trying to topple!

Hamish felt worse than ever. Now it was undeniable: it was his fault Alice had been zapped!

As the Terribles stalked round him, Hamish's mind raced.

It all made perfect sense now.

Who'd been right there when the Prime Minister had been zapped?

MYSTERIO.

Who'd invited Hamish to London straight after it happened?

MYSTERIO.

How had the Terribles known that Hamish was on Otherearth?

MYSTERIO.

'Being Mysterio got me right to the heart of power,' said Scarmarsh. 'Ten Downing Street. Right next to that silly old duffer of a PM. I knew all the comings and goings of all the most important people in the country. I had complete access! And I could rob you of the one thing you people seem to think is important!'

'Chocolate?' said Holly.

'Ego!' said Scarmarsh. 'Once I show the world that I can rob even royalty of their personalities, everybody else in the world will do everything in their power not to have it happen to them. The world will fall to me! And there'll be nothing a pair of kids can do about it!'

Hamish couldn't understand why Scarmarsh had let him come so close.

'If you wanted to zap
me,' said Hamish, 'why
didn't you do it when you
first saw me in Downing
Street?'

'With all those
journalists around?'
scoffed Scarmarsh. 'No,
no – too obvious. And, of
course, I think you may
be missing the point.'

Hamish frowned. What
other reason could there
be?

'I didn't *want* to zap
you,' smiled Scarmarsh. 'I
wanted you to come to
Otherearth. I *wanted* you
and Holly together. Why
do you think I left the
Prime Minister's diary
open? I *led* you to
Arcadian Lane!'

'I don't understand!' said Holly, but Hamish was starting to.

'You were using us,' said Hamish.

'Yes. You and your little friends. I *wanted* you here, Hamish. I *wanted* you to cause a fuss. I wanted word to spread. I've been waiting, Hamish. I let you find out I was behind the zapping. You thought you were coming here to save the King and the world – but really you were coming here to be *captured*.'

'You won't get away with this!' said Holly.

'Brave words, Holly,' smiled Scarmarsh. 'I'm so pleased you found that copy of *Evil Icon* magazine. The one with all the clues . . .'

He smiled and Holly realised what he meant.

'You *put* that there for me to find?' said Holly, the blood draining from her face.

'Do you really think Evil Icons have time to give interviews to made-up magazines? And didn't you think it was a little "convenient" that none of my Hypnobots spotted you when you were standing right in front of them?'

Holly bristled. If her arms hadn't been tied up, she'd definitely have got her RevengePad out.

'If you didn't want to zap us, then why did you zap Alice?'

said Hamish. 'She was my friend!'

'*Our* friend,' said Holly, sadly. 'Our *good* friend.'

'To give you a reason to fight,' said Scarmarsh. 'To make you angry. You were giving up and I wanted you here.'

'Why?' said Hamish. 'Why did you want to capture us?'

'Because you're bait,' said Scarmarsh. 'That's all you've been since the beginning. A little worm dangling in the river to catch a fish.'

Hamish didn't understand. Scarmarsh leaned down until he was just centimetres from Hamish's face. He was going to relish this.

'What is more likely to bring a father out of hiding, Hamish,' he said, with a stomach-churning smile, 'than the misguided belief that he can save his son?'

The words hung in the air.

Oh, no. It was all so clear now. Scarmarsh wanted to trap Hamish because what he was really after was Hamish's dad! He thought if he had Hamish then his dad – Belasko's Agent of the Year – would be forced to come to the rescue.

How could I have been so stupid? wondered Hamish. He'd endangered his best friends and now he was endangering his dad. He felt dreadful.

And then *furious*.

281

Furious at the world as much as he was furious at himself.

He pulled at his constraints, but they'd been tied too tight, and a Terrible **HUR-HUUUUR**ed a raspy chuckle.

'Just because you zap a few people doesn't mean you'll scare the rest of us into doing everything you say!' said Holly. 'We'll rise up against you!'

'Oh, sweet Holly, nice try,' said Scarmarsh, slicking her hair down with his clammy palm. 'But, as soon as your mother and Hamish's father are out of the way, there will be nothing to stop me from moving . . . to the Next Step!'

Oh, no. Elliot had been right, that day back in his war room! There's always one final, secret next step!

'Zapping the leaders was just the beginning,' said Scarmarsh. 'Eventually, I will zap *every single person on the planet*. Because once I've zapped you all . . . I can make you do *anything I like!*'

Pah! Rubbish! thought Hamish.

'No you can't!' he said. 'Everyone just walks around like halfwits! What use are they?'

Scarmarsh smiled his creepiest smile yet.

'Why do you think I call my metal friends "*Hypno*bots"?' he said. 'Once someone has been blanked, they are mine to control! Watch!'

Scarmarsh stepped over to a giant screen on wheels. It was massive. Hamish could only see the back of it until Scarmarsh spun it round.

On the screen was a picture of everyone in Downing Street. They were sitting at the Prime Minister's big table, staring blankly.

'HYPNOBOTS!' yelled Scarmarsh. **'MAKE OUR DOWNING STREET DUNCES DANCE LIKE CHICKENS!'**

The Hypnobots in the Post Office Tower all raised their arms. Their eyes began to flash and spin. A rising hum got louder and **LOUDER** and **LOUDER** . . .

The lights in Downing Street started to flash and fizz. Immediately, every single person, including the Prime Minister, stood up and danced like a chicken!

But a really weird chicken. One with constipation.

'NEXT!' shouted Scarmarsh, and now there was a shot of a packed Piccadilly Circus. Blank-eyed men and women stood still and aimless. **'MAKE THOSE PICCADILLY PEA-KNUCKLES ALL SLAP THEIR OWN BOTTOMS!'**

The **HUM** got louder still . . . Hamish could feel his fillings vibrating.

And then everybody in the whole of Piccadilly Circus began furiously slapping their own bottoms. *Slap-slap-slap-slap-slap!* The sound of bottom-slapping bounced right the way round London, and has there ever been a more horrible sound than that?

The camera zoomed out, and out, and out, until all you could see – all over London – were people slapping their own bottoms!

Football teams in stadiums slapping their own bottoms!

Army regiments in fields slapping their own bottoms!

Teachers in the staffroom slapping their own bottoms!

The slap of bottoms seemed to get louder as Hamish's mind raced and struggled to take it all in. The Hypnobots began to chant and clank. Hamish's world closed in on him. Scarmarsh was all-powerful! He'd be able to make *the whole human race do whatever he pleased*!

'My dad will not come here,' said Hamish, defiantly. 'He won't fall for your trick!'

'And nor will my mum,' said Holly, trying to free her hands. 'She's too smart for you.'

'They are smart,' laughed Scarmarsh. 'Belasko's top agents are the only ones who could have stopped me. But they were too scared. Those pathetic clowns went into hiding the

moment they found out what I was doing. And why? Because they thought it might keep you safe!'

Hamish took some comfort in that. If Scarmarsh was right, then Hamish's dad had gone out of love, not fear.

'But now I have you both exactly where I want you,' said Scarmarsh, in a low and frightening voice, 'oh, I'm sure they'll show their faces . . . *and* I get to zap the King. I really *am* a genius. *NEXT!*'

Now Buckingham Palace was on the screen – and it was chaos.

There were Terribles everywhere. I mean *everywhere*.

From north, south, east and west they'd come, following Scarmarsh's detailed instructions, and bounding towards Buckingham Palace to get the King.

Now they were clambering over the gates, thundering and slathering across the courtyard like mad dogs.

One scampered up a long stone column at the front of the Palace, cracking every window as it did so, so it might rip the Union Jill from its flagpole.

Down below, roaring, fearsome Terribles dressed as milkmen hurled steaming black bottles of blilk and charged at the gates with their shoulders. Those on the inside tried to slap the King's guards out of the way, these tall, brave

women in bearskin hats and bright red coats doing their best to keep the beasts at bay.

'I'd zap them,' said Scarmarsh, shrugging and enjoying himself, 'but their chinstraps deflect the beams.'

More Terribles – postmen, bakers, nurses and builders – poured into the courtyard. More soldiers ran to meet them. This was insania!

By the front doors of the Palace, Hamish could see Leona's taxi now skidding to a halt. A cloud of dust blew up behind it. His friends jumped out – Elliot, Venk, Clover, Colin, Elaine and Violet. Alice and Alan stayed in the back, blank-eyed and staring.

But where were Grenville and Greta?

Then he spotted them. Grenville was on Greta's enormous shoulders as she charged at the Terribles and tried to belly-bump them out of the way. Grenville was using the buns in her hair to steer!

'Get the King inside!' yelled Venk, as a group of soldiers ran to surround a baffled and terrified King Les, who still had his crown round his neck.

He was nearly at the door – nearly to safety – when disaster struck!

From left, right, in front and behind, an especially fuming

group of extra-nasty Terribles gathered.

And behind them . . .

CLUNK.
CLANK.
KLAB-ANK!

A giant, enormous Hypnobot towered over everyone, its eyes whizzing and whirring!

It was so much bigger than any of the ones they'd seen before. It seemed to be made up of dozens of smaller Hypnobots, all joined together by their rivets!

It was an *Ultima*-Hypnobot!

A group of frightened soldiers on horseback tried to charge at this horrible, dreadful battle robot. It saw them coming and emitted the loudest, most ear-jangling, nerve-trampling, muscle-pummelling, eye-watering, bottom-tightening . . . .
. . sound you've ever heard!

It was so loud and high-pitched you could probably hear it in China! Even if you had headphones! And no ears!

The horses bolted, and the soldiers that remained fell to their knees, clutching their heads!

Hamish could see that the King and the kids were surrounded.

His guards were plucked out of the way or batted to the ground by the screeching Hypnobot, some tossed across the courtyard like rag dolls.

It was too powerful!

Next to it, the Terribles – grunting, snurtling, huffling – were about to take off the King's crown.

'Looks like I'd better warm up the zapper,' said Scarmarsh, delighted, and signalling for it to happen.

Outside the Tower, a giant satellite dish began to creak round . . .

But the Terribles were having trouble getting the King's crown off. It was wedged round his ears. They picked him up and tried to shake him loose. They tugged and prised and tugged some more, they stretched and they pressed, but it just wasn't budging.

And then one of them did the worst thing possible.

With one hand, it held a giant nostril shut *and then it blew its own snot into its other hand*!

YEEEUGH!

It clapped its hands together and spread the messy gloop around, then slathered it over the King's head!

It was trying to *slide* the crown off and it had nearly done it!

But then . . .

'Who's that?' said Scarmarsh, pointing, and getting very agitated about something indeed. **'IS IT THEM?'**

A car was speeding into the courtyard, a long trail of orange dust in its wake.

It was roaring and zooming and now it was skidding.

Hamish's eyes widened and his heart nearly leapt out of his mouth.

It was a *Vauxhall Vectra*!

They're Here!

'THE SECRET PLAN HAS WORKED! THEY'RE HERE!' screamed Scarmarsh, running to the screen. **'GET ME THE BUTTON! I WANT TO ZAP THE KING AND THEN ZAP THE AGENTS MYSELF!'**

The Terribles bounded away to fetch their master's portable button.

'I'm sorry you're going to have to watch me do this, kids,' said Scarmarsh, but, from the look on his face, he wasn't sorry in the slightest.

Hamish looked at the screen again.

The doors of the Vauxhall Vectra sprang open and out jumped two figures, dressed from head to toe in black.

Hamish's heart swelled.

'It's Dad!' he said, and a wave of delight and hope and love rushed through his body. 'It's really him!'

'Mum!' said Holly, a smile spreading across her face as she saw the figure standing with Hamish's dad.

Hamish realised he didn't think he'd actually seen Holly smile before. But his pleasure was short-lived. His dad was in real danger and didn't even know it!

Down below, in front of Buckingham Palace, Hamish's dad and Holly's mum set immediately to work.

Oh, they were magnificent!

Hamish's dad whistled and once again the six ravens of the Tower of London took flight, circling the Hypnobot and blocking its line of sight. The enormous metal beast swung its huge arms at the birds, but missed. It stumbled backwards slightly, losing its footing.

The soldiers saw what was happening and were filled with bravery again, standing up to continue the battle. One of them charged at the Hypnobot with a battering ram, knocking it to the ground with a **KER-BLUUUUNK**.

Hamish's dad pulled out something from his jacket. It looked like a tiny hand-held satellite dish with two bright blue batteries on the back.

'What's that?' said Holly, but she didn't have to wait long for an answer.

Hamish's dad began to blast the Terribles who were surrounding the King.

Immediately, they went all blank-eyed and wobbly, like their legs had gone all soupy.

He blanked another one.

'He's using Scarmarsh's technology against him!' said Hamish.

The Terribles burst back into the room, followed by a fearsome Hypnobot pushing a little trolley. There was a big green button on top.

'**BRING IT HERE, HYPNOBOT!**' screamed Scarmarsh, moving to the window, where he could clearly see Buckingham Palace. '**NOW I WILL ZAP THEM! LINE UP THE SATELLITE!**'

Scarmarsh and the Terribles pressed themselves up against the window, enjoying every moment of this. Scarmarsh felt for the button, and rested one sweaty palm on top, waiting for the right moment to strike.

Hamish tugged at the ropes around him. He had to stop Scarmarsh from zapping his dad! But he was totally, utterly stuck! Say what you like about the Terribles, but they were absolutely terrific at tying knots.

Hamish wanted to cry. How was he going to get out of this one?

'H!' came a whisper from somewhere to his left.

It was Buster! Bella was holding open the door and keeping an eye out.

'What are you doing up here?' whispered Hamish. 'Run!'

'Not without you!' said Buster.

'How did you escape?' whispered Holly, eyes wide. 'We saw you – you were all tied up like us!'

'We had a little help,' said Buster, quickly freeing them. 'A little help from your friend.'

'GET READY TO ZAP!' shouted Scarmarsh into a radio, shaking with glee. **'HYPNOBOT – MAXIMUM POWER, PLEASE!'**

At least he said please.

'My friend?' said Hamish.

Buster smiled and pointed.

Hamish looked out of the window. Right there, right by the satellite dish as it warmed up and began to pulsate, look who it was!

'NOOOO!' shouted Scarmarsh.

Alex stood on another window cleaner's cradle, her hands on her hips, defiantly. How did she always know where to be? Hamish felt his wrist vibrate again and looked at The Explorer. The hands were all pointing at Alex, like she was a magnet or something. That was it! Alex had said she had a special way of 'watching' him. The Explorer must have a tracker inside.

But what was she doing out there?

'IT'S TOO LATE, NUMBER ONE!' said Scarmarsh.

Number One. No. 1.

Alex's codename – *No One*!

'It's *never* too late, Number Two!' yelled Alex.

Hamish thought if you could accuse *anyone* of being a number two, it was Scarmarsh.

'GET OUT OF THE WAY OR I'LL LET THE KIDS HAVE IT!' shouted Scarmarsh, and the Hypnobot stepped forward with an angry **CLANK** and cracked its metal knuckles.

'I don't understand,' whispered Holly, moving away from the chairs. 'Why doesn't he just zap Alex and then get our parents?'

She had a point. All Scarmarsh had to do was press that button. As soon as he did, Alex would be zapped and blanked and harmless.

But she wasn't budging. Was she mad? Or just really brave?

'OUT OF THE WAY RIGHT NOW, ALEX!' yelled Scarmarsh, almost pleading with her. **'I AM GOING TO ZAP THE AGENTS AND I AM GOING TO ZAP THE KING!'**

'No you're not,' replied Alex. 'Not while I'm standing here, Axel!'

This was madness! She was a sitting duck!

And that was when Hamish had a revelation.

Number One.

Number Two.

Alex.

Axel.

'ALEX IS SCARMARSH'S OTHERHALF!' yelled Hamish, so loudly and with such force that everyone turned round.

'How did *you* get free?' yelled Scarmarsh, panicking. Then he caught sight of the screen. Hamish's dad had zapped all the Terribles who were surrounding the King and was now ushering the **PDF** and Les through the doors of Buckingham Palace to safety. He was escaping! Time was running out! Holly's mum was right behind them, walking backwards and zapping any monsters who tried to get near them.

'*NOOOO!*' yelled Scarmarsh, 'Hypnobots! Line up *another* satellite!'

A second huge dish began to rotate and shake. This one was nowhere near Alex. It was now pointing straight down towards Hamish's dad!

This would be the end of the grown-ups. Just as it had been the end of poor Alice and Alan.

Which is when Hamish had an idea. An idea that was almost too unbearable to think about.

His head whipped round to see Alex, still standing outside, blocking the first zapper.

She stared back at him. She knew exactly what he was thinking.

Looking deep into his eyes, she half smiled and nodded, giving him permission.

No, thought Hamish. *I can't.*

But Hamish knew what had to be done. He had to save his dad. He had to save the world.

And, as the Terribles stepped towards him and his friends, and, as the huge satellite got ready to blast his father, Hamish made a dash for it.

'STOP HIM!' screamed Scarmarsh. ***'STOP HIIIIIM!'***

The Hypnobot clanked towards him, angry eyes whirring, and as it lurched forward its metal fingers grasped the back of Hamish's shoe for a moment . . .

But Hamish was too fast.

He DIVED for the big green button on the trolley . . .

. . . and *slapped it down!*

The Tower began to shake and shimmy.

And *shake*.

AND *SHIMMY*.

Alex shut her eyes.

And . . .

ZAP!

The brightest whitest light flashed full on round the Post Office Tower. So bright, and so white, and so light that the whole building glowed for a moment, like a massive lightsabre rooted to the ground.

Windows shook, desks rattled, chairs rolled round the room . . .

Buster smashed the fire alarm with his elbow and all the water sprinklers went off!

Well, Terribles hate water, don't they?

They began to pound around, terrified and steaming and screaming, finding fire exits and scrambling for the stairs.

Hypnobots don't much like water either, and they began jangling and juddering madly about, fizzing and sparking, circuit boards closing down, their camera shutters clicking shut like they were going to sleep. Forever!

And outside stood Alex, still on a window cleaner's swaying cradle, now completely still.

Expressionless.

Motionless.

Blanked.

Which meant that . . .

'Scarmarsh?' said Hamish, walking over to the crumpled wet heap on the floor. 'Scarmarsh?'

300

Axel Scarmarsh slowly stood up.

He stared at Hamish Ellerby.

Had Alex's sacrifice worked? Had Scarmarsh been blanked?

'I have always thought,' he said, very slowly, and so intimidatingly that Hamish and Holly held their breath, 'that I should like to take up badminton.'

The kids raised their eyebrows.

'Badminton?' said Holly, and she nudged Hamish, smiling.

It had worked!

It had *all* worked!

But there was still something left to do.

'Holly, Bella – tie Scarmarsh up,' said Hamish, his hair now soaked from the water sprinklers. 'Tie him up really well.'

'I'm brilliant with knots,' said Bella. 'Unlike somebody I know.'

'Talking of Buster,' said Hamish, 'do you think you can work out a way of reversing the zaps, B?'

Buster thought of poor Alice and Alan. Of Alex, standing in the wind outside. And of all the other people around the world who'd been blanked by this evil nitwit.

'I'll do my best, H,' he said, scowling at Scarmarsh.

He just smiled back and said, 'Badminton is such a wonderful team game!'

Down below, three miles away, Hamish's dad stared straight up at the Post Office Tower.

All of London had watched it shake and glow. The police were on their way now. The army too. And the navy. And the Blue Arrows. And Wilf, the security guard from the shop on the corner.

Hamish watched his dad's face on the giant screen, and stroked it.

His dad seemed to look straight at him, and smile.

302

Unbelievable!

Hamish and Holly ran.

They ran and they ran and they ran.

They ran not because they had to, but because, for once, they wanted to.

Hamish's heart was pounding as they picked up a couple of the bikes you could hire from street racks. He'd do anything to get to Buckingham Palace faster!

Buster and Bella had stayed in the Post Office Tower, doing their best to find a way of reversing the effects of Scarmarsh's rays, and Hamish would have stayed too – but he was too excited.

He was going to see his dad!

Buster had made sure that Scarmarsh was tied up. The last thing he wanted was to reverse the rays and let him escape. The police had made it to the bottom floor and were walking up the 842 stairs of the Tower as quickly as they could, which was not very quickly at all, to be honest, because none

of them had ever been on a stair-climbing course.

Hamish whizzed through the streets towards the palace. And as he made it into Green Park . . .

'Hamish!' came a voice. A voice Hamish had not heard in so long, but which made his whole soul sing.

There he was.

His dad. As tall as ever. Slightly crumpled.

Hamish took him in for a second because just to be able to look at him again meant everything. He'd dreamt of this moment since Boxing Day.

His dad's dark eyes. His slightly sticky-out ears. The sideburns he'd never get quite even.

'DAD!' cried Hamish, jumping off the bike. 'DAD!'

'MUM!' shouted Holly, throwing her bike to one side too.

Holly's mum stood next to Hamish's dad and kneeled down, arms wide open. The two kids ran to their parents and were swept up in the biggest, hugest hugs in the history of hugs on Earth. This Earth *and* Otherearth.

'I got here as quickly as I could,' said his dad. 'Oh, Hamish!'

His dad was breathing him in, not wanting to let him go even for a second.

'You are the bravest, most wonderful boy in the world. Well done, Hamish. You did it. You're my hero, son.'

Hamish squeezed his dad harder, tears forming at the corner of his eyes.

Holly hugged her mum just as hard.

'Scarmarsh is in the Post Office Tower,' said Hamish, wiping a tear away. 'He's tied up. Buster's trying to find the Reverse button!'

And, as he said that, a bright white pulse . . .

ZAPPED

. . . from *all sides* of the Tower.

BOOOOOOOM!

Trees swayed from the power of it. Everyone's hair lifted and settled. The zap travelled from the Post Office Tower to every corner of London.

Six hundred and eight-three miles away, in Germany, the Berlin TV tower received the zap and passed it on . . .

Eight hundred and twenty-five miles further on, in Kiev, the city's giant tower took the zap and immediately sent it far south, to the Auckland Sky Tower in New Zealand . . .

The reverse zap bounced and pinged its way around the world, undoing Scarmarsh's work, freeing the Neverpeople and their otherhalves on Earth . . .

Had it worked, though? Could it really have worked?

'Hamish?'

Hamish spun round. Opening the door of his dad's Vauxhall Vectra was . . . Alice Shepherd.

'What happened?' she said, dazed. 'Did we stop Scarmarsh?'

'ALICE!' said Hamish.

Behind her, Alan stumbled out, tripping on a stone.

'Someone needs to put up a "Tripping Hazard" sign here,' he said, shaking his head. 'Can someone find me a cone or something? We need to cordon this whole park off.'

Hamish was filled with joy. They'd done it. Really and truly, they'd done it.

Ten minutes later, to the cheers of everyone, Buster and Bella rode up on bikes. Alex had stayed behind to make sure the police took Scarmarsh away.

'Good work, everyone,' said Hamish's dad, proudly, and squeezing his son's shoulder. 'I think the future of Belasko is safe with you.'

'Can we go home now, Dad?' said Hamish, pleased that he was back to being someone's son again, rather than a sort of miniature freedom fighter.

The world was peaceful again.

'Sometimes, I didn't think I'd be able to come back, Hamish,' said Dad. 'But you made it so that I could.'

Hamish smiled.

'Does that mean we can watch *Star Wars* now?' he said, and his dad picked him up and hugged him again.

Buses tooted. Birds sang. A light breeze washed over them. It was a beautiful day in otherLondon again, and nothing was going to spoil it.

'I've only got one question,' said Hamish, thinking. 'What on *earth* was Mysterio's accent supposed to be?'

Buster laughed. Alice nearly spat out the kebab she'd found from goodness knows where.

'Elliot did say there'd be one extra bit to Scarmarsh's evil plan,' said Hamish, shaking his head. 'That's the problem with bad guys. They always think there's one last twist to be had, and—'

But, as he was about to finish, the world began to rumble and quake . . . Instinctively, they turned to stare up at the Post Office Tower. Something seemed off.

'No,' said Holly's mum, gravely, noticing it too. 'It's not possible . . .'

The very top of the Tower now began to vibrate and shake.

Huge blocks of concrete started to tumble from underneath it. Windows were splintering. Satellite dishes falling.

'What's happening?' said Bella. 'Is it destroying itself?'

Now it began to twist. The top of the Tower was pulling away from the rest of it! The world got noisier as a great

CCCCHHHHHH filled the air.

More concrete fell as clouds of dust formed round the Tower's shaft. Huge, fiery boosters – like the ones you get on the bottom of a space shuttle – flapped out and began shooting flames . . .

And the top of the Post Office Tower detached *from the rest of it!*

'Scarmarsh!' said Hamish's dad. 'He's escaping!'

The top of the Tower hovered for a few seconds, right there in the air – a building floating above London!

And then those boosters fired harder, and the Tower began to rise, rise, rise!

It shot off with a *BOOM*, straight up in the air, high above the city, getting smaller and smaller and smaller as it headed towards the very edge of space . . .

Scarmarsh was *gone*.

That Went Well!

'Hello, and welcome to a very special edition of *Question Me
Silly*,' said Elydia Exma, looking straight into the camera.
'Which for the second time comes to you from the small
town of Starkley.'

Everyone had turned up.

It was a week later, and this was going to be a really special
day.

For *lots* of reasons.

When Hamish and his dad got home to Starkley, his mum
had been at the door with a chocolate Mustn'tgrumble and
a shocked look on her face. As the Vectra pulled into the
driveway, she'd dropped her cup of tea and run for the car.

'JIMMY!' she shouted, not quite believing it herself.
'JIMMY, DAD'S HOME!'

Jimmy bolted from the door and the four Ellerbys hugged
each other, tight.

Jimmy kissed Hamish's hair.

'You brought Dad home,' he said. 'Thank you, Hamish!'

Hamish's dad smiled and pulled out a small plastic bag.

'I remembered the ice cream,' he said. 'Sorry it's a bit late, Jimmy.'

Now here they were – the Ellerby family – sitting in the town square, right in the front row of the audience for *Question Me Silly: A Celebration*.

Alex was here. Scarmarsh may have escaped thanks to a Terrible who'd worked out how to use an umbrella and braved the water sprinklers, but the moment the zap was reversed, Alex abseiled down the wires of the cradle, seconds before the Tower took off.

Here was brave Alice too. And brave Holly. They now got on like a house on fire. Alice had even convinced Holly she didn't need that RevengePad any more. And, now that her mum was back, Holly didn't feel she needed it either. That was the old her. In fact, she'd replaced it with a ComplimentPamphlet.

'It's a small book in which I write down nice things people have done for me so I can do something nice in return one day,' she told Elaine.

'Why?' said Elaine.

'Because . . . oh, never mind.'

There was Buster too. And Bella. And Clover. And Colin. And Alan, and all the members of the **PDF**.

Above them, the six ravens of the Tower of London swooped and cawed.

Even King Les the Second had dropped by, with a very special announcement: from now on, Starkley would be known as *Royal* Starkley!

But, as he wasn't the King in this world, no one really knew whether to take that seriously or not. So it was lucky that when the Queen arrived, and saw the signs had already been done, she rolled her eyes and said, 'Go on then . . .'

As the cameras rolled, Prime Minister Ernst Ding-Batt cleared his throat, stroked his impressive beard and stood up.

'Not for the first time, our world has been saved by some of the bravest children on the planet,' he said. 'And I say that as a very tall man indeed, who owns a poodle.'

'Show us your pants!' yelled Madame Cous Cous, cheekily.

'And as I talk to the world today,' said the PM, ignoring her, 'on this programme, which is being beamed all over this Earth and whatever other Earths there may or may not be, thanks to the wonders of some very big towers and satellite dishes, I would like to say one thing . . .'

Everyone waited for the one thing he was going to say. Hopefully, it wouldn't be about his undercrackers again.

'And I would like to be *absolutely clear* about this,' he said, pointing an important finger.

Everyone waited for him to be absolutely clear.

'And let me be clear, when I say *absolutely clear* – I mean clear in the most absolutely clearest way possible . . . and not *un*clear in any sense of the word or phrase!'

He looked at Hamish.

'*Thank* you, Hamish and friends, from everybody on the planet. Each of you has different strengths. You used them together for the good of man and womankind.'

'Imagine having a *man* Prime Minister,' said Holly, shaking her head. 'Will wonders never cease?'

And everybody applauded.

Hamish sat on the grass of the town square with his friends as King Les the Second started the karaoke.

The world was back to normal.

Except for the fact that a King from another dimension was doing karaoke.

But anyone who'd been blanked by Scarmarsh simply picked up where they'd left off. The Minister of Defence no longer spun round in her chair all the time. Vapidia Sheen got a new job hosting *Britain's Brainiest Boffins and Brainboxes*. That newsreader stopped crying because no one would buy him a pony. And the head of the army came to his senses immediately.

Although one week later he *did* end up buying a cat and calling him Poopy.

Hamish's dad sat down on the grass with him. He pulled a Chomp out of his pocket and handed it to his son.

'Thanks, Dad,' said Hamish.

He was so pleased to be able to say that again. And to have someone to play Boggle with at night.

But he still had a question.

'Dad, are you . . .' He paused because he didn't quite know how to say it. 'Are you back for good?'

His dad smiled.

'There might be times when I have to disappear for a while,' he said. 'The fight continues.'

'With Scarmarsh?'

'Not just Scarmarsh,' said Dad. 'But his masters.'

'His masters?' said Hamish, horrified.

His dad made a comforting face.

'You know how I always used to say I was "in sales"?' he said, and Hamish nodded. 'Well, let's just say Scarmarsh was in "middle management". There are also what are known as "Superiors". We've been fighting them since the Before. Now is the Now. And as for the Then . . . we'll wait and see. Scarmarsh was desperate to impress his Superiors. They knew what he was up to, but they won't let him fail again. The Superiors want to take our world, H. We can't let them.'

'When you say "we", do you mean Belasko?' asked Hamish.

'When I say "we", I mean you and me, pal.'

His dad looked up into the sky.

'You see, Starkley isn't all that it seems,' he said. 'The town has a secret. One which even the Superiors don't know yet. It's all to do with the town clock . . .'

But, as interesting as that was, Hamish had already stopped listening.

Because he'd noticed something very strange happening.

He'd put his Chomp down on the grass. But now it was sort of twitching.

He stared harder, and it twitched once more.

A big twitch.

Why was a Chomp twitching?

'Dad,' he said, but his dad was still talking about whatever he was talking about. 'Dad?'

What the *heck*?!

The Chomp was now a couple of centimetres off the grass. It was levitating!

Hamish looked around. There was an empty can of Cherry Pepsi by a bin . . . but it wasn't on the ground. It *had* been because Hamish had seen it and made a mental note to put it in the bin.

But now that can was . . . sort of floating.

He felt The Explorer start to pull upwards on his wrist, and watched as his arm rose, involuntarily.

What was happening?

His dad kept talking, and Hamish scanned the town.

Hey – what was that? Did a leaf just shoot up into the air?

His friend Robin had been doing headers with a football nearby. But now he just stood and stared, as his ball kept climbing high into the sky.

To his right, someone screamed. The bag of shopping they'd been carrying was now floating away, like a balloon on the wind.

'My squirrel!' yelled old Mr Neate, as a bewildered Hans-Joachim got caught in a tree.

'Dad,' said Hamish, tapping him, urgently. 'LOOK!'

A whole *car* was starting to rise upwards . . .

Shop signs were straining against the nails that held them down . . .

All the sweets in the window of Madame Cous Cous's International World of Treats began to ping out of their positions, splattering one by one on the ceiling.

All over Starkley, sensing something was wrong, people started to dash indoors as they felt themselves beginning to rise into the air.

Only the town clock stood still, unaffected.

'Oh, no,' said Dad.

'What is it?' asked Hamish, panicking, as his dad grabbed him and pulled him back towards Lovelock Close.

'It's a GravityBurp!' said his dad.

'What's a *GravityBurp*?' asked Hamish, confused.

'A sort of energy blip that messes with the very laws of nature for a moment or three,' his dad replied. 'You see, Hamish, the fight isn't over! What are they trying *this* time?'

And, as they burst through the front door of their house to find both Mum and Jimmy completely flat on the ceiling and *very* confused, for the second time in his life, Hamish Ellerby knew one thing.

That every end . . .

. . . is just another beginning.

THE END

Or is it . . . *THE BEGINNING?*

HAMISH ELLERBY SAYS THANK YOU

Town hero Hamish Ellerby has done it again! But before he can do anything else at all, he insists on saying his thank yous (because he has been very well brought up).

His first thanks are for Mrs GE Wallace, Master EB Wallace and Miss CE Wallace of the Wallace family, Wallaceford. You all stink.

From Otherearth, he'd like to thank special agents Mrs Roberta Kirby and Mister Ari-fella Feiner for their kind attentions. Also singled out for particular praise was award-winning local marketing guru Elias Offord. Door-to-door salesman (Starkley and Frinkley) Laurence Hough also received a firm and manly handshake. Huge thanks to everyone at Simone & Schuster too.

But even bigger thanks are due to oddball doodler Janie Littler, designer of the year Paulette Coomey, and the editor's editor Jeff Griffiths.

And Hamish's final and biggest thanks of all – go to YOU!

Tweets   Tweets & replies

Jimmy Ellerby @jimmyellerby · 1m
OH ACTUALLY IT IS A PE

Jimmy Ellerby @jimmyellerby · 2m
WHAT THE HECK IS THIS

Jimmy Ellerby @jimmyellerby · 2m
HANG ON IT'S NOT A PEAN

Jimmy Ellerby @jimmyellerby · 2m
I JUST SAW A PEANUT

Jimmy Ellerby @jimmyellerby · 3m
HAMISH'S ANOTHER STUPID

Danny Wallace @dannywallace
ALERT THE CHILDREN OF THE WOR
very soon... #HelloHamish #February

Jimmy Ellerby @jimmyellerby · Oct 26
HALF TERM HALF TERM
HALF TERM HALF TERM

Jimmy Ellerby @jimmyellerby · Oct 26
HAMISH'S STUPID BOOK

Travelcard

UNORTHODOX LINE
<<ARCADIAN LANE>>
Valid for all
eternity

No down escalator at Dog Walk Station until 2059

NONNE SCITIS

1026. DICTIONARY OF SPA

Gravity: What keeps your feet on the ground

Gravityburp: Momentary blip that alters gravity

Gravityburper: Legendary device used to manipulate the laws of physics

Gravy: What you put on your chips

OTHERLONDON TOWN PLANNI

Chief Planning Officer

```
To: All
From: Cindy Bing


Um... so has anyone noticed that the top of the Post Office
Tower has gone missing? Only it's not there any more.
Apparently it just shot off into space. Oh well.
Anyway, Terry's come up with some ideas for what we can
replace it with before people start talking, because you know
what people are like.

1.   Terry says the top of the tower could just be a giant
     light bulb. (We could dim it at night)
2.   Terry says the top of the tower could just be an enormous
     disco ball (although this means we would be a committing
     to a permanent 24-hour disco).
3.   Terry says we could just keep quiet and hope no one
     notices.

I don't think Terry is very bright.
```

GBC

New to GBC1!
The all-new...
Life's a Dream with Vapidia Sheen

Episode 1: Vapidia solves string theory

Episode 2: Vapidia writes a complicated Spanish opera by accident

Episode 3: Vapidia asks "Why does the predicted mass of the quantum vacuum have so little effect on the expansion of the universe?" – with hilarious results!!!

The award-winning
Sonny Griffiths
and his
Ridiculous
Yellow Ukulele
New album out now!

Includes the songs
"What a Beautiful Nose Your Dog Has"
and
"Excuse Me, Are You Belgian?".

INSIDE!

Sergeant Major Gets Cat – Calls him 'Mr Poopy' page 5

New Pants Dance p3 – learn the craze that's sweeping the nation!

p132 NASA – Giant Object Spotted in Space. Seems a Little Sinister

PROUD ORGAN OF BRITAIN'S LEAST MOST BORING TOWN

Starkley Post

2st Friday 2016 issue XXI vol 8

PRICE £9

EVERYTHING'S UP IN THE AIR!

In a startling turn of events, the office of the Starkley Post was in turmoil today when literally everything in it started to float into the air.

"I only noticed when a rubber began to gently nudge my nostril," said editor Rhona Framp. "And then it shot straight up there! I've got a rubber up my nose!"

Presumably some scientist or other is looking into things. Hopefully one will look into Rhona's nostrils.

Until then, can someone please send help as we're all stuck on the ceiling and no one can reach the phones.

Claim Your FREE Seeds
– Grow a Venus Fly Trap inside. p97

NAME: DANNY WALLACE

Danny Wallace is an award-winning writer who's done lots of silly things. He's been a quiz show host. A character in a video game. He's made TV shows about monkeys, robots, and starting his own country. He has written lots of books for grown ups, in which he uses words like 'invidious', and he pretends he knows what they mean but he doesn't. He thinks you're terrific.

DANNY
WALLACE

NAME: JAMIE LITTLER

Jamie graduated from the Arts Institute at Bournemouth in 2008 and won a High Commendation in the Macmillan Children's Book Award. When not trying to tame his unnaturally fast growing hair or having staring matches with next door's cat he likes drawing, colouring in, cutting things out and sticking things in.

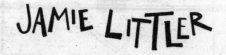

JAMIE LITTLER

Go to **worldofhamish.com** NOW to find out more about Hamish and Danny, join the PDF, watch exclusive videos PLUS the chance to enter special competitions!

OPPERS